Two Friends, Too Old

Two Friends, Too Old

Robert Scott

Fresh Ink Group
Roanoke

Two Friends, Too Old

Fresh Ink Group
An Imprint of:
The Fresh Ink Group, LLC
PO Box 525
Roanoke, TX 76262
Email: info@FreshInkGroup.com
www.FreshInkGroup.com

Edition 1.0   2012

Book design by Ann Stewart

Cover design by Moonfire

Cover art by Moonfire

Cataloging-in-Publication Recommendations: General Fiction; Crime (Fiction); Psychological (Fiction); Suspense (Fiction); Medical (Fiction); Family Life (Fiction); Friendship; Aging Issues; Dementia

Library of Congress Control Number: 2012940677

ISBN-13: 978-1-936442-11-9

To my grandson Dylan, who while hiking with me many years ago said, "Grandpa, tell me a story," and thus began my journey into fiction.

Acknowledgements

I wish to acknowledge the contributions of the "Monday Authors," a group of writers whose kind and thoughtful critique of this story improved it immeasurably.

Chapter 1
The Gravel Pit

"I hadn't planned to go out this way, you know, Frankie. Not this way at all."

Clay seemed pretty calm, seeing how he was staring into the barrel of a 12-gauge shotgun I was holding, not more than ten feet away. He was so close that I couldn't see all of his face, only from the eyes up. The rest was hidden by the sight at the end of the barrel and by the barrel itself. There was no hiding his ears, though; they stuck out like wing flaps. Clay could wiggle his ears, and he did so sometimes on the weirdest occasions, like when he was saying his marriage vows or thinking of just the right phrase to silence an obstructionist when he was presiding over a Chamber of Commerce meeting. Clay's ears were distinguished by another physical aspect; they had so much white hair it looked as if he'd just come in from a blizzard. The amount of hair on his ears always amazed me because he was completely bald on top, and had been since his thirties. And his baldness contrasted too with his facial hair. Clay didn't have a five o'clock shadow; his always appeared before lunch. And it was evident now, white stubble mixed with flecks of gray and black. Looking at him, one got the impression that two different sculptors had been involved with his head, one starting on the top, the other on the bottom, each totally oblivious to what the other was doing.

I aimed right at the scar in the middle of his forehead, the one he got when he threw a block for me in that high-school football game, the one for the state championship. The block knocked his helmet off, and he got kicked in the head falling to the ground. Clay rolled up and ran into the end zone to give me a big hug, blood running down his face and him grinning from ear to ear as if to say, "That was fun, let's do it again." That was not the first block Clay had thrown for me, nor the last. He was always tough, been tough as a railroad spike ever since I first saw him, from that opening day in kindergarten when the teacher moved Clay to the front of the room so she could keep an eye on him. She sat him down right in front of me and as soon as she turned her back, Clay twisted around in his seat and gave me a big grin. He hadn't softened up much in the sixty-plus years since.

"So this is where you're planning to do it, right here in the gravel pit. It's as good a place as any, I guess, seeing as what else we've done here."

I didn't say anything; right then I didn't have much to say to my best friend. I had said it all before, and the time for talking had passed. When I didn't respond, Clay went on. Maybe he thought I would change my mind if he kept talking, because he started in on the weather.

"At least you could've picked a better day. I haven't seen it this miserable since I don't know when."

He was right about the weather. It had been raining on and off since dawn, a steady rain that would let up for 20 minutes or so and then return. There were puddles of rainwater in the gravel pit, although right now it was just misting. Thunderheads covered the western sky, and every three or four minutes they showed flashes of lightning. I could tell they were headed our way because the roar of the thunder had gotten louder since we stepped out of the pickup. A gray day, more rain was on the way soon, not atypical weather for the first week of November. I automatically counted the seconds between the lightning and the thunder, thinking maybe I could time my shot so the noise would be covered by thunder. A brighter flash of lightning caused Clay to instinctively turn his head to his left. With his head still turned, Clay looked at me cunningly out the corner of his eye, seeing if I was watching the lightning and not him. I wasn't; the sight at the end of the barrel was now over the hole in his right ear. The ear was wiggling. Clay swung his head back, and the gun sight returned to the scar. He looked at me straight on, tugging on the bill of his Molson County Co-op hat.

"What are you gonna do with my body? Have you thought about that?"

"See that concrete over there?" I said, gesturing with my head toward a jumble of cement blocks the size of small refrigerators. In addition to using this spot to store gravel, it was the dumping ground for pieces of abutments from the bridge the county replaced last year.

"The key's in that front-end loader; I checked it out yesterday. No one from the county will visit the gravel pit until they need sand to put on the roads when it snows. By that time they won't be able to remember exactly how all the concrete was dumped, and it will be twenty years or better before someone starts messing around with those blocks and you turn up. By that time I'll be long gone."

Clay was silent for a moment, giving that prospect some thought. Both ears wiggled rapidly.

"Well, what are you gonna tell people about what happened to me?"

"After we're finished here, I'm driving to Middleton, park a couple of blocks away from the bus station, and buy a ticket clean through to Florida, just like you told everyone you were doing. I'll get off in Junction where they change drivers, take the next bus back to Middleton to pick up my rig, and drive home. If anyone asks, the bus driver will say one old guy bought a ticket to Florida and, as far as he knows, that's where he went. They don't know either one of us, and they can't tell one old guy from another. I'm not worried about anyone waiting for you at the other end 'cause you told me you didn't pre-register. Said you'd sign up when you got there. If anybody asks me, I'll tell them I drove you to Middleton and put you on the bus. The last I saw of you, you were headed down the road. No one will ever suspect me."

"Thought of everything, haven't you? Then, you've always been the smart one, going to that Ivy League law school and all."

"Smart enough," I said. "Smart enough."

Neither one of us said anything for a minute, and then Clay spoke up. "You've known her, what? Six, seven years? I've known you longer than that, Frankie boy, a way lot longer. We go too far back for this. It's not right, you being the one to do this to me. It's just not right."

"Shelley turned seven last month. What's not right is you. You had your chance, and you didn't take it. It's your fault, Clay; it's all your fault we're in this gravel pit."

I could hear the anger rising in my voice. There was fear, too, because I'd never done anything like this before, and sadness, as well, because it was the end. The fear and the sadness made me weak, but the anger made me strong and the anger was more powerful. I glanced at my watch. I had to leave soon to catch the bus.

"It was that boat. We never should've gone to look at that boat." Clay dropped his head; there was a hint of resignation in his voice.

Clay was wrong about the boat putting us in the gravel pit. The boat thing was the end of the deal; the beginning was before. When you've known a guy all your life and seen him practically every day, you don't miss stuff like this; you just don't.

It began last spring, right around the middle of March.

Chapter 2
The Beginning

I'd driven over to Clay's place for no particular reason. That day I was out running errands for Lucille, picking up things, dropping things off. It was too early in the afternoon to go back home, especially since Lucille had been dropping hints lately that I was getting underfoot all the time since retiring the first of the year. The weather was chilly but clear, giving a hint of what spring would be like once winter had given up the ghost for good. No one was saying it was spring now, that would jinx it for sure. But you could tell everyone was thinking spring was just around the corner; they were more upbeat than they had been just ten days ago when the heavy, black clouds of February hung so low you felt you had to stoop over whenever you went outside. Getting out of my pickup in Clay's driveway, I heard Clay swearing and a dog howling from the back. I hustled around the corner of his house to see what all the ruckus was about. What I saw stunned me.

Clay was beating his golden retriever, Mollie, with a piece of rebar. He had tied Mollie to a tree and was swinging the rebar like a baseball bat. The dog was spread-eagled on the ground, almost motionless, just twitching a little. Clay was methodically pounding Mollie, hitting her from head to tail in a steady rhythm. His biceps, hard from a lifelong regime of twice-a-week weightlifting, bulged out from a white T-shirt soaked in sweat. Every thud of the rebar against Mollie's prostrate body produced a gasp of exhalation from Clay. I couldn't believe my eyes. He had had this dog for over ten years, best dog he'd ever had, he always said.

"Clay, what's going on here?"

He looked up. The expression on his face was so frightening I took a step backwards, my feet getting tangled up, stumbling around, almost falling down. For what seemed like five minutes but, looking back, was probably only five seconds, Clay didn't say anything. Then his face softened, returning to normal.

"Mollie had rabies, had to be put down."

"Had rabies! Since when? You never told me that. Last week she was fine when we were walking down by the river."

"This weekend. She got 'em this weekend. Had to put her down. Didn't want her biting any kids in the neighborhood."

"Clay, why didn't you take her to the vet?"

"Had to do it myself." Then Clay smiled at me, the same smile I'd seen all of my life. "Say, I bet you came over for some of my cinnamon rolls. Come on in. They should be just about ready to come out of the oven."

He didn't wait for a response, just leaned the rebar against the back porch and went inside. I didn't move from my spot, trying to figure out what I had just seen, not quite able to put all the pieces together. It just didn't seem to make any sense, Clay saying Mollie had come down with rabies so suddenly. I looked over at her; Mollie lay still, no movement at all. She was dead, no way she would still be alive after all that beating.

I don't know how long I would have stood there replaying the scene in my mind, maybe the rest of the day; but when I heard the back door open, I turned toward the house.

"Frankie boy, are you coming in or what? The rolls are cooling on top of the stove. Get in here."

Clay was standing in the doorway, wearing an apron. That was the second weird thing I saw that day. I looked back at Mollie. There was nothing I could do for her. I wanted to believe that she had rabies and that Clay had not gone around the bend, but his kitchen told a different story.

Clay has never been what you would call a neat person. In fact, it would be a compliment to call him "messy." Picture a whirlwind going through a room on an hourly basis, and you would get a pretty good idea how he lived. His wife, Donna, used to keep him in check, but since her death last year it was like a dam had burst. To find a spot to sit in his living room, I usually had to move clothes or books or newspapers, fishing equipment, or a wrench from a chair. Last week when I was in his kitchen munching down on a sweet roll I'd brought over, there was a small drill press on the table, a skill saw on one chair, and a tool box on the other. The guts of a chain-saw engine were scattered across the counter top. But this morning Clay's kitchen looked like it was ready for a photo shoot for a kitchen magazine.

There was a spotless tablecloth on the table, and two place mats and cloth napkins that matched the tablecloth. Coffee cups and saucers from Donna's china cabinet sat in the middle of the place mats alongside spoons from her silver service. The counters sparkled, not a single dirty fork to be seen. A matching set of kitchen knives hung in precise order from a wall next to the sink. Inspecting Clay's kitchen, I don't think there was a toothpick out of place.

Clay was looking in a cupboard when I started to sit down at the kitchen table. He half turned around and grabbed me gently by the arm.

"Here, Frankie, sit down over here. This is where you need to sit," he said, guiding me to another chair at the table.

I sat down where he wanted me to, but I couldn't see any difference. I must have had a quizzical look on my face because Clay tried to explain his kitchen-table seating arrangement.

"This is where guests should sit, on this side of the table."

I looked around again, maybe I was missing something. It was a different view of the kitchen all right, but basically I was looking at the same thing, white kitchen cabinets. I was closely examining this side of the kitchen when Clay put a cup in front of me. It held hot water, with a tea bag.

"Clay," I said with a note of astonishment in my voice, "when did you start drinking tea?" Clay was a coffee drinker, always had been, and not particularly good coffee at that. Whenever I needed a container to hold nuts or bolts, I'd go over to Clay's and retrieve an empty two-pound coffee can from his garbage can. He'd been drinking the same brand for over thirty years. And I don't think he'd ever had a mocha or a latte in his entire life.

"Ordered this off the web two weeks ago. Just came in the mail yesterday. It should just be about ready," Clay said, scooping the tea bag out of my cup with a miniature spoon lost in his catcher's mitt paw of a hand. "Here, try it with a little lemon and milk." He pushed a tiny bowl of lemons toward me and set a small pitcher of milk on the table. I tasted the tea—not bad. Not that I would switch from coffee, but the tea wasn't that bad. I could see where a guy might get used to drinking it every now and then.

And those cinnamon buns, that was a big shock, too. As far as I knew, he'd never cooked anything. He always said he hated to cook and that he was no good at it. On our hunting and fishing trips, I did entirely all of the cooking. I refused to let him cook because he was terrible at it; he was so bad he even burned hot water.

Chapter 3
Frank Decides to Act

Over the next couple of weeks the image of Clay beating his dog recurred more than once in my mind, and I wondered what exactly was going on with him and whether it was a one-time thing. Whenever I was around him, I found myself looking closely at him, seeing if he was weirded out or something. There were a couple of things I hadn't noticed before, but I couldn't tell if they were new, or if they had always been there and I just hadn't seen them because I hadn't been looking that closely. I had pretty much made up my mind that the thing with Mollie was a one-off event—until the jaywalker encounter.

I was riding with Clay on our way to look at new fishing flies at Moe's Bait and Tackle Shop, gearing up for fishing season starting that weekend. We were having a heated conversation about what fly worked best for the evening hatch on the river. He favored a Royal Coachman; me, I was backing a little brown Nymph. I asked him how he could be so sure, and he cited as authority his neighbor's sister's husband.

I countered with my Lucille's uncle's son. Clay was telling me how that guy didn't know a dragonfly from a fruit fly, when suddenly he said, "Whoa," and brought the car to a stop.

About thirty feet ahead, a teenage boy of about sixteen had stepped out from between a couple of parked cars and was starting across the street. Although it was a warm day in April, the kid was wearing a stocking cap. He had a sleeveless T-shirt on, and his long shorts hung so low their ability to stay on his body defied the laws of gravity. The boy had an i-Pod in his hand, and was taking his time juking his way across the street. He was far enough ahead of us that Clay hadn't had to slam on the brakes, and we weren't thrown against the dashboard or anything like that. I was just waiting for the kid to get by us, but not Clay.

Clay rolled down his window and laced into the kid, stringing together in one sentence more profanity than I thought was grammatically possible; I was kinda impressed with my best friend's ability to swear. The longer he went on, the redder his face got, and his breath started coming in gasps. Clay kept on after catching his breath, and I was thinking, *What in the world has got into him; what's the big deal?* The kid would have just kept walking across the street, ignoring us, except that Clay laid on the horn. He turned, looked right at us, and then gave us that impassive "whatever" look that teenage boys have perfected by the time they're fifteen, a look that infuriates adults because they know they are defenseless against it. I thought that would be how it would end, a staring contest between Clay and the kid, but then the kid rolled his eyes. Clay jammed the gearshift into park and put his hand on the door handle.

I reached out to put my hand on Clay's shoulder, and was within a couple of inches of touching him when something told me not to. I jerked my hand back like I had just grabbed a hold of an electric fence.

"Clay," I said loudly and sharply. No effect.

Clay pushed down on the door handle, and the door started to open.

"Clay," I said again, this time louder. "Clay, I've got to get right back home after we look at flies. Lucille's expecting me to watch Shelley." Clay stopped, his body rigid, except for his ears. His ears were wiggling rapidly. Nothing happened for the next ten seconds, and then Clay's body relaxed.

"He's not worth it," Clay muttered under his breath as he pulled the door closed and shifted into gear.

That night eating dinner by myself in the kitchen, Lucille having gone to a church meeting, that scene in the street with Clay and the kid kept running through my mind. That was not like Clay, not at all. People never upset him, even if they acted poorly. Especially kids, he had generally cut them a lot of slack, always reminding me how we were growing up. I might have been able to put down the deal with Mollie as just a bad day—who knows what Clay was going through the first year after his wife died?—but the thing with the kid, I couldn't ignore that. Then there was his spotless kitchen and the thing with the tea. That made four things, five if you counted him wearing an apron. I have no idea what a psychiatrist would call it, but it seemed to me that Clay was weirding out. And what would have happened between Clay and the kid if I hadn't been there? I ran a couple of scenarios through my head, keeping in mind what had happened to Mollie, and every scenario turned out bad, some really bad. Never mind the kid; they would have been bad for Clay. That's where I left it when I went to bed that night, but it was with me the next morning.

In fact, it was the first thing I thought of immediately upon waking up, and it was about the only thing I thought of that day and the next and the next. A deal like this, it sort of crowds everything else out until, without knowing exactly when, you've come to a decision. It's like turning a corner without realizing a corner is there. I kept thinking somebody had to do something about Clay until it dawned on me I had decided that that somebody was me. Clay had other friends, but none as close as me. Maybe I thought because he was my best friend, I owed it to him. Maybe I was tired of this thing weighing down on me and didn't want to waste time trying to get other people involved in it. Maybe I didn't want to embarrass Clay by him knowing I had told others about his behavior. Maybe I thought I would be better than anyone else to solve this problem and wanted to be the one to do it. But deciding to do something is way different than deciding what to do. I had a couple of restless nights thinking how best to approach Clay—until he helped out.

Chapter 4
Frank Fails

A week or so after the thing with the kid, we were in his den, each nursing a beer we'd opened during half-time of a football game on television. The mid-April weather had turned miserable; the wind was up to 20 miles an hour, blowing sleet sideways. Winter was taking one more good run at us here in the high plains section of the Midwest. ESPN2 was replaying the Super Bowl. Neither one of us was particularly interested in the game, but no way you'd want to be outside on a day like this. Clay was in his pantry looking for some chips during a long commercial break and my eyes roamed around his den, landing on a faded photograph stuck in a picture frame.

It was a photo from a newspaper article, of Clay and me in our high-school baseball uniforms. He was wearing his catcher's equipment, and the photo showed us shaking hands. The caption read, *Clay Barnard congratulates Frank Henry on pitching a perfect game to win the Class A State Baseball Championship.* The caption had it backwards. I was congratulating Clay on calling a perfect game. The whole game, including the two extra innings, I never shook his sign off, not once. And he was dead on with each pitch. Earlier in the season I learned the hard way never to question Clay's pitch selection.

It was the top of the ninth inning in a game against Sperline. We were up by one run, and there were two out with a runner on second. I had two strikes on the batter, and wanted to finish him off with a fastball. I figured I had enough juice left in me to blow one by him, feeling bullet-proof the guy could never hit my smoke. Clay kept signaling for a curve ball and I kept shaking him off. Finally he gave up and gave me the sign for a fastball. The batter drove it over the left-field fence. Clay didn't say anything when he walked out to the mound and handed me a new ball, he didn't have to. In the bottom of the ninth Clay hit a towering home run over the center field fence, driving in the runner on first and winning the game for us. He saved the game for us and in the process enabled me to go the whole season without posting a single loss. I never shook him off after the Sperline game, never questioned his decisions from that point on, and I know his pitch-calling was a major reason we went undefeated that year.

"Hey, Frankie, have you seen Mollie around? Haven't seen her for a couple of days," Clay said, returning to the den and putting a bowl of chips on the floor between us. "Can't figure where she is, she couldn't have run off."

I didn't see where I would get a better opening so I grabbed this one.

"You killed her, Clay—beat her to death with a piece of rebar. Couple of weeks ago. You told me she had rabies, but I know she didn't. There was nothing wrong with Mollie; she didn't have rabies. You had gotten her shots for rabies. You were always telling me what a great dog she was, never gave you a single problem. How long had you had her? Ten, twelve years, at least?"

Clay gave me a blank look, like what I was telling him wasn't registering. He blinked a couple of times and then looked down at the floor. "Fifteen. Got her as a pup. She would be fifteen this coming October."

He couldn't keep eye contact. He'd look at me, then immediately look away, like he didn't want me to look at his eyes. I thought maybe he didn't want me to see tears welling up in his eyes, but that wasn't it. I saw his reflection in the mirror above the fireplace. It wasn't sadness in his face I saw, but fear, stark fear. For someone who played college football against guys who outweighed him by fifty pounds and had gotten two Silver Stars in Vietnam, I'd always considered Clay immune to fear up to now. He was rubbing his right hand over the knuckles of his left, so hard and fast I was sure he'd wear the skin off.

"The other night, after dark, I was standing at the sink, washing the dinner dishes. I was looking out the window, and I don't know what happened, but I saw myself hitting Mollie with a piece of rebar. It was like I was outside my body, watching me hit her. I wasn't feeling bad about doing it; in fact I didn't have any feelings at all. The whole thing happened so fast I couldn't wrap my mind around it. I just put it down to nothing, just one of those random thoughts you get every now and then that doesn't mean anything. But this one wasn't random. This one means something. What does it mean, Frankie?"

I cleared my throat to give me time to come up with an answer. Then the lawyer in me kicked in. When all else fails, tell the truth. It may be brutal, but the truth will come out anyway, and with a lie the listener will have to deal with two bad things: the brutal truth, plus the deceit.

"Like I said, Clay, you killed her. Beat her to death with rebar. Before I went home that day, I went into your garage, got a shovel, and buried Mollie out behind your compost pile. I didn't want you to see what you had done."

I threw the rebar into Mollie's grave as well, but I didn't tell Clay that. I wasn't sure how much he could handle, where he was mentally.

Clay stopped rubbing his knuckles. He didn't move a bit. I wasn't even sure he was breathing, he was so still. I didn't say anything; he didn't say anything, but there was no silence. The jumbled thoughts ricocheting around in my head drowned out the TV announcer. Clay's brain was just as noisy; you've been with a guy since kindergarten, you know these things, you just do. I tell you, though, it was agony for me to sit there and see him in such pain.

"You're a good friend, Frankie. A guy couldn't ask for a better friend. I should've taken care of Mollie. She was my dog, and it was my job. But you did it for me, and I won't forget that."

"Clay, you think maybe you should see someone? Maybe talk to some professional." I offered this advice gingerly, unsure how it would be received.

"You think I'm nuts, Frankie? Off my rocker?" I was glad there was no anger in Clay's voice, only a tone of honest inquiry, tinged with more than a little fear. Now we're getting somewhere, I thought.

"No, Clay. I don't think you're nuts. Nothing like that. I just think it would help if you could talk to someone."

I could see Clay was turning this prospect over, looking at it from all angles with his analytical mind, the same mind that made him the most sought-after CPA in this part of the state—the same mind that had people clamoring for him to be president or chairman of every volunteer organization in the county, particularly those that were on the verge of going under. Clay had rescued and resuscitated everything from the Humane Society to the Homeless Shelter. The three times he headed United Way, it set records. Once, he had generated so much over the goal that an entire new wing of the hospital could be built.

"Who would I see, Frankie?"

"Well, there's the folks over at Mental Health."

"I'm on their Board of Directors. I'm on the advisory committee for the psych ward at the hospital, too. I've done the taxes for every psychologist and half the counselors in town, at least all of the good ones. I don't think I can tell people I've known for years I beat my dog to death with a piece of rebar."

"Okay. Okay. I can see that. We'll just look in the yellow pages for Thurston. It's over three hours away, and no one knows you down there."

"You're right. No one knows me in Thurston."

I could see Clay was mulling over the Thurston idea. He looked up, not at me, but out the window, into the distance.

"I can't do it, Frankie. I can't go to Thurston. I can't tell a stranger what I did, someone I don't know. That doesn't know me, who I am, what I'm about."

"Let me get this straight, Clay." I could feel myself getting a little angry because he wasn't making any sense. "You can't talk to anyone in town because they know you, and you can't talk to anyone out of town because they don't know you. Am I getting this right?"

Clay didn't say anything for a moment; then he spoke. "Yeah, I guess. That's about the size of it, I guess."

"Clay, it's like you're in the bottom of a well, the water is rising, there's rope to the top, right next to your hand, and you won't grab it, won't pull yourself up. What's going on here? This is crazy."

"Yeah, maybe. I don't know. That's just how I feel."

I didn't leave it there. We argued through the second half of that football game and through a couple of major league exhibition baseball games. Around five in the afternoon I called Lucille and told her I wouldn't be home for dinner. Didn't exactly tell her why, just said I was catching some games with Clay. She was okay with that.

We weren't drinking much beer. I only had two, and I think Clay didn't even finish his second one. I came at him from every point of the compass, but I couldn't get him to budge. Once, the excitement in the announcer's voice caused both of us to turn toward the TV. There was a replay of a touchdown catch. Where the thought came from I don't know; it just popped out.

"Clay," I said softly, "what if next time it's not a dog, but a person, a human being? What happens then?"

He started to speak, then paused. Then he spoke. "He was in. It was a touchdown. No way he was out of bounds."

I didn't say anything, thinking there would be more. But there wasn't. That was it.

We kept on going right through the ten o'clock sports round up. By eleven, I was exhausted from arguing with Clay. Only, it was more like arguing *at* him since he never responded to the points I made or tried in any way to counter them. I repeated my arguments so many times I got tired of listening to them. That didn't seem to bother Clay at all. He didn't get angry or irritated or tell me to mind my own business. When I was being emphatic about some idea, he would swivel around in his chair, listen to me without interrupting, nod his head to acknowledge he'd heard me, and then turn back to the TV. Every now and then he would make some noncommittal response. More than once I came close to throwing a beer can at him. When I got up to go home, he walked with me to the door and told me good night, using the same words he'd used for forty years. I drove home one part tired, one part discouraged, and one part mystified. And mad— mad, too, because my best friend from forever was headed for a train wreck, and he was the engineer, hand on the throttle, pushing it all the way down.

Chapter 5
A New Idea

And that's about where matters stood until two days later when I accidentally supercharged Lucille's tuna casserole with some picante sauce. About an hour before suppertime I was in my shop sharpening the blade on the lawnmower, getting ready for the first mow of the spring, when the phone rang. It was an old rotary phone that Clay had pulled out of the dump. The two of us hooked it up to the telephone line. In those days the phone company charged you extra if you had a second phone in the house, but we figured that they had got enough of our money, so we never told them about this phone. The hook-up was in the back of the house, so they never saw it. Came in handy when we wanted to do a little business and saw no reason to bother Lucille with it. It was her on the line.

"Frank, I'm not gonna be home for dinner. We're gonna head over to the nursing home to visit Aunt Dora, and then we're gonna go out to eat at that new Chinese place. Always wanted to try Chinese food, and this is my chance, seeing as how you would never take me there. Be home around eight-thirty or nine. There's a tuna casserole in the freezer you can put in the microwave and enough fresh vegetables for a salad. And remember, you've got to turn on the microwave; you can't just put it in there and expect it to defrost. I don't know what's gotten into you lately. The other night I came into the kitchen and you were staring at the microwave like you were waiting for something to happen on its own. I think you would have been there until bedtime if I hadn't started it for you. Sometimes I think your head's not screwed on tight. Well, anyway, I'll see you when I get home. Have a good evening. And for crying out loud, turn on the microwave!"

Lucille hung up before I could acknowledge receipt of her instructions. I went into the kitchen, found the casserole, and nuked it the microwave. Lucille not being home, I ate it right out of the bowl. The first two bites were bland, and that's when I went for the picante sauce, which I found way in the back of the refrigerator. I dumped a good portion of it on the casserole and then for good measure added another large dollop. About a half hour later, as I was putting the dishes in the dishwasher, my stomach started to rumble like a volcano and then began to heat up like one, too. That drove me into the medicine cabinet where the Tums were. Getting the Tums out of the cabinet, I knocked a pill bottle off the shelf and it fell into the sink. Picking up the bottle to return it to the shelf, I noticed the prescription. The pills were for Hal, Lucille's father, who passed away around six months ago. Lucille, having grown up hearing her parents talk constantly about the Depression and them never throwing away any-thing that might possibly be good, must have grabbed the pills when she and her siblings cleaned out Hal's house before they put it up for sale. She probably put them in our medicine cabinet thinking they just might come in handy sometime. A year ago in January, I'd had a brief but rather intense involvement with his pills. Standing there in the bathroom and seeing those pills again brought back vivid memories of that encounter.

It had been an early Saturday afternoon around the middle of the month. I was standing at the living-room window watching the snow fall. More than a half of foot of snow had come down during the night, and right then it was snowing so hard that the street lights had come on. I was trying to convince myself that it was too soon to shovel the walk—it would get just get all covered up again right away—when I heard the phone ring in the kitchen. Lucille answered it.

"Frank," Lucille said, walking into the living room after hanging up the phone, "that was Barney. Said he was plowing his driveway and saw Dad drive into a ditch, on a perfectly straight road. Dad's pickup was stuck in the snow bank so bad Barney couldn't pull it out, so he took Dad back home. The reason he called, he said, was Dad was acting kinda weird. Said that Dad mentioned something about going to town to get some pills, and Barney wondered if he had gotten off some medicine or something. I wonder if he needs a refill. I bet that's it. I bet he's out of the pills that Hal, Jr., prescribed for him. I wonder if we should do something."

The "we" was me because there was no way Lucille would be driving today.

"I'll get a refill from Matt and take Hal's pills out to him," I said. I started suiting up for the weather.

I chained up the 4X4 all the way around, slung four 50-pound sand bags in the bed, and for good measure threw a snow shovel in the back, as well. Driving into downtown toward Matt's Pharmacy, I didn't see any lights in the stores. On Main Street only a bar showed any sign of life, its neon beer sign blinking brightly through the snowfall, a beacon for the early afternoon drinkers. I pulled up in front of the pharmacy. No sign of life there, I thought, and grabbed my cell phone to call Matt.

"Hello," said Matt, answering on the first ring.

"Matt, Frank here. I think Hal's out of pills, and I need to take a refill to him."

"Frankie, my car's stuck in the driveway. Tried to get out but couldn't even make the street. Don't know what to do. It's too far to walk in this blizzard. Can't remember when I've ever seen it this bad. There's got to be more than a foot of new snow on the flat now."

I knew Matt was stuck. If there were any way he could open up today, he would. It wasn't that he hated to miss an opportunity to make a nickel, but he was very conscientious. As the only pharmacist in town, he knew people needed him to be open. I'd known Matt since high school, although he was two years behind me. When I was a senior, we were both on the debate team. He was one of those people who seemed to melt into the crowd, nothing special about him, nothing that made me think at the time he would amount to anything remarkable. Turned out I was wrong; turned out Matt was one of those individuals a community could use more of.

To begin with, he became one of the wealthier people in town. He and his brother inherited the pharmacy from their parents and, after a year, Matt bought out his brother. The pharmacy turned out to be a real cash register, being the only one around for fifty miles. By looking at him, you wouldn't know Matt had money. He drove a 10-year-old car; he didn't shop at Goodwill, but he was only one step up from that; and his house, although well-kept, was nothing special. He never married, so didn't have kids to send through college. I never heard he took any exotic vacations. Word in town was Matt was an "accumulator," just kept accumulating property like some people collect stamps. He bought a fair number of old buildings in town and fixed them up. That really spruced up downtown. Matt leased the buildings to various businesses, and he had a reputation for being a good landlord, fair with the rent and quick to make needed repairs. As a result he had a very low turnover rate in his tenants.

On more than one occasion he'd helped out the community financially when some volunteer effort was in a pinch. And each year for the past fifteen years he'd single-handedly funded two full college scholarships for graduating seniors. No one in town was aware that he was behind these scholarships except the principal and me. Matt never liked to make a big deal of his financial help; once he told me he didn't think it was anything special. The only reason I knew about it was because I drew up the legal papers for the scholarship. Over the years, I'd done quite a bit of legal work for him, mostly regarding property matters, but I'd also drawn up his will as well as the scholarship. More than once we had a long chat about things in general after we had settled the legal work he'd brought in. I enjoyed those conversations, and I think Matt did, as well. He was a good client, and I always looked forward to seeing him.

"I'll come and get you, Matt. Monday I put my plow on the pickup, just in case. Turns out that was a smart move. Need be, I'll plow my way to your house."

"Okay, I'll be watching for you from the living room."

Matt was out his front door before my pickup rolled to a stop in his driveway. As he climbed into my truck, I could see he was dressed for the weather. A black navy watch cap was pulled down over his ears, and his down parka was zipped up to his chin. Fleece-lined jeans were tucked into the top of his felt-lined boots. When he pushed up his cap with his mittens,

I could see the hollows in his cheeks were red from the cold, walking the fifty or so feet from his house to my rig.

"You picked up on the first ring, like you were expecting my call," I said, backing out of Matt's driveway and following my tracks back downtown.

He didn't answer immediately. Matt was like that. He was weighing his answer. Not that he was trying to think of the right thing to say. It was more like he was deciding which words to use to convey exactly what he wanted to say using no more words than absolutely necessary. He wasn't taciturn, just very efficient with words.

"Weather like this," he started, "people get nervous. Don't know how long the storm will last. They start thinking they might run out of things. Yours was the fifth phone call I got, wanting to know if I was open or not. You were the first who could get me down there. I'll give those other folks a call when I get to the store, tell them I'll be open all day, just like usual. The town plows Main Street and a couple of side streets, they'll be in."

I was going no more than five miles an hour. I didn't want to put on the brakes because I could tell the road was slick underneath. I wasn't concerned about hitting another car; there was no one else on the road. But I might slide off the street and hit something and maybe damage my pickup so it wouldn't run. I didn't want that to happen. I turned onto Main Street and headed for Matt's store, three blocks down. I looked over at Matt, and he seemed to want to tell me something.

"What do you know about the stuff Hal is taking?" he said.

"Miazanton. Not much."

"Miazannon," Matt corrected. "Miazannon," he repeated. "When Hal, Jr., prescribed it, I had never heard of it, so I read up on it. Read the flyer that came with the medicine and then went on the Web to do some more investigation."

"You do that with all the drugs you sell?" I said, interrupting him.

Matt was silent for a minute and then started up again. He looked straight ahead, like he wasn't talking to me, but to someone else. We were just creeping down Main Street now, barely moving at all. It was quiet in the cab of the pickup; I could hear the tires crunching on the newly fallen snow, the low whirl of the heater, the *swish, swish, swish* of the wiper blades.

"First year after I got my pharmacy license, right after I graduated from State, ol' Doc Hastings called in a prescription for Mrs. O'Doul. Took the call myself. I hadn't heard of the drug he prescribed so I mentioned to my dad I was going to check into it. He was still working then; we were working together. Dad said, 'Check into it, what for? If the doctor prescribed it, that's good enough for us.' Said if I wanted any information about medicine, I could just read the flyer that came with it. So I did, just read the flyer. Nothing much in it, and I gave Mrs. O'Doul the pills when she came in."

Matt hesitated, like he was waiting for me to say something. I had an idea what Matt was about to say, but it was his story to tell, so I let him do the telling.

"You remember Jennifer O'Doul, don't you? The only person born in Springdale with flippers for arms. The medicine was Thalidomide. After I heard about what happened to Jennifer, I re-read the flyer that came with Thalidomide. Didn't say anything about birth defects. Then I went to the library and started reading newspapers that had come out a couple of years before she was born, to see if there were any reports about Thalidomide. Turns out that there were several articles about kids born with birth defects in Europe, just like Jennifer. After that, every time Mrs. O'Doul came in the store, I ran and hid in the back. That worked until dad died, and then I had to face her. Funny thing, she never blamed me, not at all. Was always really nice and friendly to me. When I heard that she died, and then Jennifer passed away a couple of years later, well, I felt a little relieved. Maybe I shouldn't have, but I did."

Matt was catching his breath between every sentence; I thought maybe he would start crying.

"Wasn't your fault. Doc Hastings was the one who pre-scribed it. Sounds like you were following normal procedure."

"I was the one who pushed the drug across the counter to her, the last person in the chain. The information was out there; I just had to make the effort to get it, and I didn't bother. So as time went on, bit by bit I started reading up on every single drug I sold. I started just with the flyer, but with the flyer you can't get a real good idea what a drug can do, what the real likelihood is something bad will happen. The drug companies use a shotgun approach when they describe side effects, throwing everything in, including the kitchen sink. A person gets lulled into a false sense of security or gives up with so much information. But now with the inter-net there is a lot of stuff out there that is really good, but you have to decide for yourself if it is reliable. I've been doing it for long enough now I think I've got a good handle on it, and that's how I found out about Miazannon."

"What about Miazannon?"

"It's both a benefit and a curse." A benefit because it works great, gets old folks acting normally. They stop being angry, don't try to hit people anymore. Calms 'em right down."

"That's why Hal was taking it," I interrupted. "He was getting ugly mean, pushing people around. Even Lucille. Left a mark on her cheek one time when he hit her. If she hadn't jerked her head away just in time, probably would have broken her jaw as hard as he was swinging. Good thing Hal, Jr., was a doctor and got him on those pills. Calmed the old man down right away. What's wrong with them?"

"The curse is that once you're on it, you've got to stay on it. If you stop taking Miazannon, you fall back. Not to just where you were before you started taking it, but worse. You get really wacky, start acting bizarre, doing things way out of normal. The stuff I've read says it's totally unpredictable what might happen. But getting off it doesn't affect all people the same. For some, there's no effect at all, and for others, well, it's pretty bad. I read where one guy attacked a complete stranger. Was really beating him up until some passerby pulled the guy off. But it doesn't always happen right away when you stop taking the stuff. Sometimes it does, but not always. It could happen later, days, even weeks."

I must have had a puzzled look on my face because Matt went on.

"Look, Frank, think of it this way. Using Miazannon is like a finger pushing down on a spring. Pushing the spring down past its starting point represses whatever caused the aggressive behavior in the first place. Everything is okay as long as your finger is on that spring. But once you get off Miazannon, the mechanism that has been repressed springs back higher than it was to start with."

"Why doesn't the government take it off the market?" I asked.

"The stuff on the internet is from doctors or relatives about what happened to someone who stopped taking Miazannon. The manufacturer is running press releases attacking the stuff on the internet, saying their drug is perfectly safe and all these adverse effects are the result of something else. The FDA hasn't done anything yet; I don't know why. Probably nothing will change until you guys start suing them."

"Yeah, maybe you're right," I said, pulling into a parking spot in front of the drug store. Matt unlocked the front door and we went in, leaving a trail of snow as we walked past the greeting-card counters. He disappeared through a door behind the pharmacy counter, and a second later fluorescent lights came on, one row at a time, a wave of light starting at the back wall, advancing toward me, and then over me until the entire store was bathed in brilliant white light. I heard Matt rustling around in the shelves behind the counter, and a minute later he reappeared with a large bottle in one hand and a smaller one in the other.

At the counter Matt up-ended the larger bottle and beige-colored pills spilled out. He counted out thirty-five pills and put them in the small bottle.

"Giving you an extra five in case Hal's a little slow in getting around for a refill. These guys are pretty pricey, fifteen dollars each. Funny, though, my cousin's sister runs a pharmacy in Canada, and I was talking to her one day about this. Told me she sells this stuff for five dollars a pill because the Canadian government buys all the prescriptions in bulk. Gets a volume discount. She said the same is true in Great Britain and Europe. All those governments buy in bulk and get a volume discount. The Part D law makes it a crime for our government to buy in bulk, so no one in the US gets a volume discount. Big Pharma said if the US government got a volume discount, companies wouldn't have enough profit to pay for research and development. But the way I see it, no one in Canada or Britain or Europe is paying for any research, only us here in the United States. Those guys are getting a free ride, and we're paying for it."

I slid my debit card over to Matt, and he ran it through the machine. Nothing happened. He ran it again. Again, nothing happened. Matt stared at the machine and then spoke.

"Line must be down. On account of the snow. You're good for it, though, don't worry."

"Better have me sign something or we'll both forget."

Matt dug around in a drawer and came up with an old receipt book, one with carbon paper for the store copy. He wrote on it and pushed it across the counter to me.

I signed the receipt, took my copy and pushed the receipt book back to Matt.

Matt held the pill bottle in his hand; I thought for a second he wasn't going to give them to me. Then he opened his hand and placed the bottle on the counter, but closer to him than to me.

"Make sure Hal takes those pills, and make sure he doesn't run out. You promise?"

For a second that struck me as a little strange, Matt making a customer promise to take pills. Then I realized where he was coming from.

"That O'Doul girl, Jennifer, you did all the law required. You're not to blame for what happened to her."

"Tell that to Jennifer. There's more blame than what's in those law books of yours, Frank. There's the blame you take to bed with you at night."

The bottle of pills was still on Matt's side of the counter. He wasn't making any move to hand them to me. I reached over and put my hand on them. Matt put his hand on top of mine, firmly. I looked up from my hand and into Matt's face.

"I'll see that Hal takes his pills, every day. I'll see to that."

Matt took his hand off mine. I unzipped my jacket and slipped the bottle into my shirt pocket. Neither one of us spoke as I zipped up, put my gloves on, and went out the door into the snow storm.

Chapter 6
They Worked Good on Hal

I got out to Hal's place just as daylight was fading, busting through some snow drifts and using my plow to make my way through others. Just before turning into his quarter-mile long driveway I passed his pickup, nose down in the ditch, back end sticking straight up in the air. The wind had drifted the snow halfway up the driver's-side window. The direction the wind was coming from, I figured the kitchen entrance would be in the lee, so I headed in that direction. Opening the door and stepping inside, I saw Hal sitting at the kitchen table. Barney wasn't exaggerating; Hal had really lost it.

A woman's hat, black and decorated with lace, perched precariously on Hal's head, and shaving cream covered his cheeks and throat. His wire-rim glasses hung from just one ear, and a strap of his overalls was off. In the front pocket of the overalls where pencils usually go, Hal had stuck knives, forks, spoons, and a whisk. Under the overalls was a clean white shirt, perfectly ironed, and a bolo tie with the slide pushed clear up to his neck. A work boot all laced up was on one foot and a tennis shoe was on the other. Both hands were on the table, palms up.

I said, "Hello," but it didn't register. With a thousand-yard stare in his eyes he looked right through me. I got the impression that as far as Hal was concerned, I wasn't there. My next move was instinctive. I pulled the bottle of pills out of my shirt pocket, snapped the top off, and dropped a pill in one of his hands. There was a glass on the table, half full of water, and I pushed it close to his other hand. For about ten seconds nothing happened; and then in a robot-like manner Hal mechanically raised to his mouth the hand containing the pill and rolled it in. He started to gag and gulped down some water. All this time Hal looked straight ahead; I don't think he ever saw the pill or the water. It was like he was on auto pilot, which was fortunate for me because I had no Plan B.

I took a chair across the table from Hal and watched to see what would happen next. I kept my coat on and my back to the door. I guess I was prepared to bolt if something dangerous happened, but it didn't. After about fifteen minutes Hal's face started to soften and the glaze began to leave his eyes. Ten more minutes passed and he blinked a couple of times, like he was waking up. Then he brushed his hand against his chin.

"What the hey?" Hal said, his hand coming away covered with shaving cream. That's when he noticed me.

"Frank, when did you show up?"

I hesitated before answering, concerned if I told Hal I'd been sitting across the table from him for the better part of a half hour, he would dispute that and get angry. Or he would be upset realizing he had been disassociated from reality. Remembering Matt's comments about the unpredictability of someone who goes off Miazannon, I did not want to do anything that might set Hal off. So as much for his safety as mine, I shaded the truth. "Just now walked in the door," I said.

Hal got up from the table, walked over to the sink, and washed the shaving cream off his face. He sort of staggered back to his chair, slumped down in it, and put both elbows on the table, resting his head in his hands. "Man, I'm beat. Feel like I've been bucking hay all day, and every bale ran to more than ninety pounds."

"Well it's about time to turn in," I said, glancing at my watch. It read 7:30, but it was pitch black outside, so I thought Hal wouldn't know it was still early. I figured if I could get him into bed he was less likely to harm himself or anyone else, like me.

"Yeah, I guess you're right. Time to turn in. See you in the morning."

For about a minute he didn't move, and I thought he'd changed his mind. Then, with a grunt he pushed himself upright and a little unsteadily climbed the stairs to his bedroom, the hat falling off in the process. After a couple of minutes I heard his bed creak—and then nothing. I figured Lucille would be anxious about what was going on, so I gave her a call and filled her in.

"Well, good, Frank. Sounds like you've got things pretty much under control out there."

I could hear the relief in Lucille's voice. "Yeah, I think so, too. But I'm going to stay out here at least for the night to make sure everything's okay. And besides, I don't want to be driving back to town in this weather. Tomorrow should be better. On the way out the radio said the storm should taper off by midnight."

"Okay, but look, Frank. If Dad starts acting strange or getting out of hand again, you hightail it out of there. Don't try to deal with him; it won't work. Don't take any chances. I know he's got guns in the house, at least two rifles and a couple of shotguns. Sleep in the bunkhouse tonight. It's got a good wood stove and there're sleeping bags out there. It's not your thing. It's my thing, and Hal, Jr.'s, and my sister Sally's."

"Okay," I said, "I'll check out the bunkhouse." I hung up, thinking it might not be my thing, but I'm the one who's out here, not Hal, Jr., not Sally, not Lucille. I'm the one in the barrel, the one who's going to deal with Hal if anything happens.

That night I stayed in the bunkhouse and locked the door from the inside because I didn't know what Hal might do. Contrary to the radio, the storm did not let up during the night. It was going full bore when I woke up about 6:00 the next morning and beat my way through eighteen inches of snow back to the house. I started a fire in the wood stove in the living room and then went back into the kitchen to make some coffee. I was just sitting down with my first cup when Hal came into the kitchen. I didn't know what to expect and didn't exactly know what to do, so I did the first thing that came into my mind. I handed him a cup of coffee. He sat down and drank the entire cup without saying a word. I poured him a second cup and put a pill right next to it. Without any comment Hal put the Miazannon in his mouth and washed it down with a swig of coffee. I went to the stove to make some scrambled eggs for the two of us, positioning my body so I could keep an eye on him while working the eggs. Hal was pretty quiet during breakfast, but by lunch-time he was almost normal. I was on my guard most of the day, pretty much just following his lead, not even making any suggestions to him because I didn't want to set him off. We did a couple of chores together, packing in some firewood from the wood shed, reorganizing the food in his pantry, sorting stuff for recycling. By supper he was close to 100%.

As I was washing up the dishes after eating, I looked out the window and saw the snow was letting up. In the distance a yellow light blinked on and off, so I knew the county snowplow was working the road. I called Lucille and talked over with her whether I should come home in the morning. She said if I thought Hal was all right it would be okay for me to leave. The next morning Hal was fine, and I left right after breakfast, first seeing he took another pill.

After that Lucille and I made sure Hal never ran out of pills. And the Miazannon did its job; Hal never once gave us a bit of trouble after that day in January.

Chapter 7
Frank Tries Again

I looked at the bottle of Miazannon sitting in my hand and saw it was almost full. I thought of Hal and the pills. Then I thought of Clay and the pills. Then I shoved the bottle into my pants pocket and headed downstairs to the computer in the rec room.

I'd lucked out because Internet Doctor had a couple of pages on these pills. Reading through three pages of disclosure and disclaimers, I came to the symptoms Miazannon was designed to cure. Some of them fit Clay to a tee. I grabbed the phone and dialed his number. He picked up on the first ring.

"Clay, are you doing anything right now? Lucille's gone for the evening, and I thought I might come over to shoot the breeze."

"Nope, just picking the lint out of my belly button. Come on over. I should be done by the time you get here." I wondered if Clay used that line on anyone else; I never heard him.

"Okay, I'm headed out the door now. Be there in five."

After he pushed a cup of peppermint tea across his kitchen table to me, I said, "I've been thinking about what we talked about last Saturday when we were watching football. You know, about your dog and all."

"Yeah, what about it?" Clay said with an even tone in his voice.

"Well, you remember Hal, Lucille's dad. How for a while he was acting a little . . ." I struggled to find the right word, the one that would convey the point I was trying to get across without setting him off. "A little different, you know. Remember me telling you one time he even tried to hit Lucille? Well, Hal, Jr., you know, Lucille's brother who's a doctor over in Meridian, prescribed some pills for Hal, and that settled him right down. Got him back to normal, like he always was. I just found some of his pills when I was going through our medicine cabinet tonight looking for some Tums and thinking about Mollie and, well, you know . . ."

My voice trailed off. I took the bottle of pills from my coat pocket and set it on the kitchen table in front of Clay.

He reached for the bottle and turned the label toward him. Clay studied the label for way longer than it would have taken him to read it. Then he raised his head and spoke. "You practicing medicine now, Frank? Now that you're retired from the law, you're taking up medicine? Not any downside to these, is there, Frank?"

I can't remember the last time Clay called me Frank and not Frankie. I had a vague feeling it was when he was calling me on something, something real important. I can't remember what it was, but it seemed it didn't turn out too good for Clay. But I wanted my best friend back so we could keep on doing the things we'd always done, the things we'd planned as we were heading into retirement, things I was really looking forward to.

"Yeah, Clay, I'm sure those pills will do the trick. I went on the Web and read all about them. It's just what the doctor ordered. When those run out, we'll go see Jimmie, tell him what the deal is, how you were acting and how those pills worked, and he'll give you a prescription of your own."

I wasn't 100% positive Jimmie would prescribe these pills for Clay, but I was pretty sure. Jimmie had grown up with Clay and me, played football with us from seventh grade on up, guard right next to Clay as a tackle, and generally hung out with us all through school. He went off to medical school and came back to town to set up his practice here. The three of us still did things together on occasion. We were close, not as tight as Clay and I, but still pretty close.

Clay looked at the bottle again. "I want to get back to normal. Lord knows I do. I look down the road and I can't see anything; nothing's in focus. I can't stand myself, knowing what I did to Mollie."

He paused, started to say something and then stopped. Then he twisted the lid off and dumped one white pill into his gigantic hand. It sat in a crease, looking not much bigger than a grain of rice, and just as innocent. I thought maybe Clay wouldn't take it; he looked at it so long. Then he opened his mouth so wide I could see the back of his throat, and with one swift move he tossed it in, washing the pill down with a swallow of tea.

I stayed for another forty-five minutes or so, generally shooting the breeze, exchanging gossip, telling stories, and went home thinking we had hammered that coffin shut tight. I hadn't got around to telling him about not stopping the pills. The right time just didn't seem to come up in our conversation. Anyway, I told myself driving home that night, Matt would give this information to Clay the first time he went in for a refill. I could count on Matt for that, for sure.

Changing into my pajamas that night I found myself wondering if I had violated any laws, me giving Clay Hal's pills. I wasn't a pharmacist or a doctor, so none of those laws applied to me. I hadn't taken any money from Clay for the pills, so it wasn't like I was trafficking in drugs. I had just given a friend some leftover medicine. People do that all the time. Technically that might be against the law, but no one ever gets prosecuted for it. And besides, I thought, climbing into bed next to Lucille, it was the only option I had.

Jimmie turned out to be no problem at all. Packing a half rack of beer, Clay and I showed up at his office one Friday night just at quitting time. I knew Jimmie had no plans for this Friday night, or for any other night for that matter. He had just gone through a nasty divorce and was pretty much by himself these days. Three beers into the rack I could tell Jimmie was getting a buzz on as he related how the judge had given him the short end of the stick in his divorce case. He was getting up a good head of steam about how the law was pretty much a joke when I saw my opportunity and hit him up about prescribing Miazannon for Clay. With his current lack of respect for the law, it didn't take much convincing to get Jimmie to sign a prescription for Clay, with twelve monthly renewals.

Driving back home that night I wondered whether I should have advised Jimmie to do an examination of Clay before writing him the prescription for Miazannon. That's what the law required. But then I thought, Jimmie was a doctor with more than thirty years of experience; he didn't need me telling him what the law was on this point. And besides, he wasn't my client; I didn't owe him any duty.

The Miazannon did the trick; I had my old Clay back. He even started drinking lousy coffee again. Things were back to normal, or so I thought until that Saturday in November when I went looking for a fishing boat.

Chapter 8
The Three Musketeers
Take a Road Trip

"Think that old beater can haul a boat?"

I looked up from inspecting the right front tire of my neighbor Leonard's '79 half-ton Chevy. Clay was walking up my driveway.

"Thought you had a dentist appointment or something today," I said.

"Was gonna have a filling replaced, but the office called and said Helen had just gone into labor. I don't want anyone but her drilling on my teeth, so I took a pass on the other dentist there. Didn't have anything better to do, and thought you just might need some help shopping for your boat. What you know about boats would fit in a thimble, and there'd be room left over for . . ."

The back door of the house opened up, and Lucille stepped out, followed by my granddaughter, Shelley. I shot Clay a warning glance, and he stopped talking.

"Remember, Frank, it's a number-nine quilting needle. Not a number eight, not a number ten, a number nine."

Lucille spotted Clay.

"You're helping Frank shop for needles this morning, Clay?" There was a hint of suspicion in her voice. Clay did his best to convince her that his being at our house was completely innocent.

"Just trying to avoid yard work at my place, Lucille, just trying to avoid yard work. But if you think Frankie needs help shopping for your quilting needles, well I'm willing to lend some assistance in that venture."

Lucille rolled her eyes and then stooped down to talk to her granddaughter.

"Shelley, you keep an eye on your grandpa and Clay. I'm counting on you to keep them out of trouble, and I hope to almighty heaven you're up to it. And Shelley, remember you have to work on your spelling words."

"I'm a pretty good speller," Clay said. "Why don't you go get your spelling words, Shelley, and I can help you with 'em while we do errands today."

My granddaughter darted back into the house and, seconds later, re-emerged with a sheet of paper in her hand. "Here they are, Grandpa Clay. I can do most of them, but the ones at the bottom are kinda hard. I want to get a hundred this time. Last time Jennifer beat me by one, and I want to beat her this time. She's the only one in the second grade that wins me, and I don't like her anymore, not at all."

"Oh, Shelley, don't say that. You know Jennifer is one of your best friends. You always want to go next door to play with her when you come to stay with us. Or she's over here for a sleep-over with you. You know you like her."

"That was before she won me. I like spiders better than her."

Lucille rolled her eyes again, giving up the argument. "Well, anyway, make sure you work on your spelling words. Frank, I'm going over to the nursing home to see Aunt Alice and then over to Emma's to quilt. I don't know when I'll be home, maybe around eight o'clock tonight. Supper is in the refrigerator. There's enough for you, too, Clay. All you have to do is put it in the microwave for five minutes. Can the two of you remember that, five minutes in the microwave and number-nine quilting needles?"

Lucille stepped back into the house without securing any acknowledgement from me, or from anyone else for that matter.

"You got all that, Clay?" I said as he lifted Shelley into the pickup and tightened her seat belt.

Clay hesitated before climbing in himself. "You sure you wanted to take this rig? It doesn't look like it can even make it to the end of the driveway."

"Jump in, Clay. It's not much for looks, but it's sure heck for stout."

"Okay, but you're the one going for the tow truck if we break down way out there in the boonies," Clay said, climbing in and pulling the door closed. I got in the other side and closed my door. Even with all of us on the pickup's bench seat, no one was pressed for space. Sitting between Clay and me Shelley did not take up much room, and with Clay leaning on his window, the three of us fit in the cab pretty nicely.

I turned the key, and the engine fired right up with a healthy roar, causing Clay to nod his head in silent approval and give me "two thumbs up." An instant later Shelley gave me the seven-year-old's version of "two thumbs up."

I could see why Clay might initially have been dubious about Leonard's truck. The driver's-side mirror displayed a diagonal crack, producing two slightly different views of the road behind. A coat hanger substituted for a radio antenna, and the gearshift knob was a fuchsia-colored solid piece of glass. The headliner was brown with a good cover of dust, and strips of cloth dangled down from the roof of the cab in more than one place. A glance at the bed of the pickup revealed a rusted-out muffler, an old tire, and the blade of a shovel. The pickup's predominate color was primer gray.

"Where's your rig, by the way," Clay asked as I backed on-to the street.

"In the shop getting the water pump replaced. Number-nine quilting needle, that's what we've got to get for Lucille. You got that, Clay? You got that?" I repeated, my first inquiry having elicited no response.

"Right here, Frankie. Right here," Clay replied, tapping his liver-spotted forehead with the knuckles of the first two fingers of his gnarled right hand. "Say, does Lucille know we're gonna be shopping for a fishing boat today?"

"That sounded kinda empty, Clay. We better write it down. Open that glove box and see if there is a piece of paper and a pen or pencil somewhere in there. And no, Lucille doesn't know. I figured no reason to mention anything to her just yet, seeing as how I might be just shopping and not buying."

Clay pushed on the button on the glove box. Nothing happened. He pushed again, same result.

"Wack it hard, with your hand."

The glove box door popped open, emitting a cloud of dust.

"Poke around in there and see if you can find a pencil and a piece of paper and write down number-nine needles. We don't want to forget Lucille's needles. We're going to have enough challenges today as it is."

"Can I try, Grandpa? Let me try. I know my letters. Is it okay if I print? I don't know how to write yet. You don't learn cursive until the third grade, and I'm only in second grade. How do you spell 'number'?"

"Here, Shelley," said Clay, handing Shelley the paper and the pencil. "Give it a go. 'Number' is n—u—m—b—"

"Wait, Grandpa Clay. You're going too fast. What comes after the 'm'?"

Clay repeated "number" and spelled "needle." He wasn't really her Grandpa, but Shelley announced one day she was adopting Clay as her "second" Grandpa. I was "Grandpa" and he was "Grandpa Clay." Clay was around the house a lot, especially since his wife died, and he had a knack of "grandfathering" her well—just the right mixture of affection, instruction, and discipline. Shelley was always asking if we could go over to see Grandpa Clay, and I had got in the habit of taking her with us when we went somewhere, like to the hardware store, to coffee, or anyplace old guys go when they're just hanging out, solving the world's problems. I could tell being with her was good for Clay, brought him out of the dumps, and he was his old cheerful, joking self when Shelley was along. He was always asking me when Shelley was coming to our house for a visit. We must have spent a lot of time together because Lucille started calling us "The Three Musketeers." I thought Shelley was pretty special, too; she was our only grandchild.

"There, that's done. Where should I put this piece of paper, Grandpa?"

"Put it someplace where it won't get lost."

Shelley was not paying any attention to me; she was intently studying the floor of Leonard's pickup.

"Hey, Grandpa! Look at the floor! You can see the road go by if you look at the floor. There're holes in it. I've never seen that before. It's really neat!"

I glanced down at the floor; the street showed through numerous holes of various dimensions.

"Clay, reach under the seat and see if Leonard's got any cardboard under there we can use as floor mats. Leonard's after-market upgrades usually consist of cardboard. We may be driving on some dirt roads to get to the guy's house where the boat is, and I don't want a dust storm in the pickup."

Clay reached under the bench seat. "I think I found some cardboard. Now if I can just get this jack handle off it, we'll have ourselves a floor mat."

Clay gave the cardboard a couple of jerks, and the cardboard slid out, bringing with it the jack handle. Bending over almost double, Clay crunched the cardboard on the floor on his side, around the gearshift, and under the pedals, covering most, but not all, of the holes. "There, that should hold the worst of it." Clay grimaced as he straightened up, his left hand going to the small of his back.

"I guess we ought to go over to Ryan's. It's on the way out of town, and it's our best shot for getting a trailer hitch."

At the mention of Ryan's, I saw Clay's face darken.

"If the old man's there, I might just give him a piece of my mind," he said, a hard look coming over his face. "I don't like even talking to him; he thinks that he's doing you a favor just by opening up every day."

"Nope, I heard at coffee the other day he's in the hospital having a knee replaced."

"Maybe they should replace his manners at the same time. This jack handle would come in real handy to teach him some manners. That would straighten him out, in a hurry."

There was meanness in Clay's voice, real meanness. I thought about giving it a pass but didn't. "Say, Clay, how's that medicine working out? Still taking it, right?"

"Nope. Stopped about a week ago. Made me feel kinda funny. Anyway, I don't need it." Clay must have sensed I was about to say something because he continued in a low voice. "I'm fine, Frankie, just fine. Not to worry."

I thought about whether to let it ride, Clay stopping his pills. Maybe I shouldn't have, but Shelley was with us and we were just starting out on an all-day adventure with everyone in high spirits, and I didn't want to spoil the mood. I was arguing with myself whether to continue the medication conversation when Shelley piped up and distracted me.

"Can we get Grandma's needles at this store?"

"No," I said, "we'll get Grandma's needles a little later. We're looking for a boat hitch."

"What's a boat hitch?"

"It's a ball about the size of a tennis ball. You put a boat trailer on the ball, and then you put a boat on the trailer." Clay was filling in the gaps here.

"Grandpa, you don't have a boat!"

"A deficiency that we plan on rectifying today, Shelley," Clay interjected as we pulled into Ryan's Hardware and Rent-All.

Shelley shot Clay a look of annoyance that said, if you want to talk to me, use words I know. Then she turned to me.

"What do you mean? Are you getting a boat today? I thought we were just going to the store to get Grandma some quilting needles."

Being my granddaughter, I couldn't shine Shelly on. That's the rule for grandpas: you can't shine your grandkids on.

"We are going to see a man about a boat. He lives way out in the country. I might buy it. Might not. I don't know. It could be old and beat up and no good. We'll just have to see. We're going out to take a look. Maybe that's all we'll do today, just look. Then we'll get Grandma's needles. We have plenty of time. We've got all day."

"Gee, Grandpa, getting a boat would be awesome. I could dive off the boat into the water, as soon as I learn how to swim."

"We'll see, honey, we'll see."

Pulling into a parking space, I shut off the engine, waited for the dieseling to stop, and then popped the door open with my shoulder and stepped out. Shelley slid across the seat toward the passenger door. Clay lifted her onto the ground and grasped her hand firmly, and we all headed across the parking lot to the store. Well, truth be told, I walked and Shelley jumped. Each time she came to a line in the pavement, she jumped over it, assisted by Clay swinging her by the hand. After her second jump, she talked Clay into joining her, and the two of them jumped their way to the front door.

"We need a boat hitch," Clay said to the teenage clerk manning the cash register.

"What size? We've got 2 ¼'s, 2 ½'s, and 2 ⅝'s."

Our first obstacle. Clay and I looked at one another, both thinking the same thing. We had no idea what size would work. There was nothing in the want ad about the size of the boat hitch needed.

"It's an old boat, an '82 Stormbeater. The trailer's probably an '82 as well." I hoped that this data would clarify matters. It did.

"If it's an '82, you'll want the 2 ⅝-inch hitch. The metal wasn't very good in those old ones, so they made 'em bigger."

I wondered how the clerk knew so much about something that was made when he was still in diapers. He sounded awful sure of himself, but then he was a teenager and they're never in doubt. He must have seen the questioning in my eyes.

"My granddad had an old Stormbeater about that same age. I spent a lot of time with him growing up, and he knew a lot about boats and boat trailers and things like that."

"Frankie," Clay interjected, "we don't know how old the trailer is. It could be the guy's second or third trailer. Maybe we should take all three, just to be safe."

"Yeah, Clay. You could be right, you just could be right. We could waste half a day going way out in the country to the guy's house only to find out we had the wrong hitch. It might be a couple of weeks before we could get back there again. By then, someone else would have beat us to it." I turned back to the clerk. "Yeah, better give us all three, just to be on the safe side."

"What about lights? You guys have brake lights and turn signals for the trailer? I've got a kit that will work for any pickup. Only $43.20 a day."

With renting three hitches I would be pushing my budget, but we could be coming back after dark. From the sound of the ad, the trailer lights probably did not work. "Sure, throw in the light kit. We might just need it."

"With something for the governor, the damage is $87.37," announced the clerk as he filled out the rental contract.

As I was signing the contract Clay put two twenties and a five on the counter. I looked at him.

"I figure that will buy me a couple of fishing trips on that boat of yours," Clay said with a grin. I grinned back at him and matched his contribution.

"You pick up the change and you're buying lunch."

"Fair enough," Clay said, scooping the change into his pocket.

He picked up the light kit, and I struggled out the door with the three heavy boat hitches.

We headed east out of town, away from the mountains and into the sagebrush and scab rock country. An hour later I turned off State Route 3 and onto a narrow asphalt county road with crumbling shoulders, frequent pot holes, and no center stripe. We were soon rolling across an undulating landscape marked by sagebrush, brown bunch grass, and columns of basalt. The only signs of civilization were the telephone poles carrying two strands of wire. I guessed one was a phone line and the other was for electricity. Every now and then there was a solitary wooden fence post, generally leaning forty-five degrees to the ground and dangling a single strand of barbed-wire. We lost most of our sun soon after turning onto the county road, and a gray overcast now ran from horizon to horizon. From time to time rays of light poked through the clouds, shining off spider-webs that covered dead bunch grass. It looked kinda cold out there, and I bet it was. At 6,000 feet elevation, this high desert plateau can turn cold in the first of November, especially with a little bit of moisture in the air.

I kept looking around at the landscape, half listening to Clay and Shelley working on Shelley's spelling words. They were in a heated discussion about how to spell "photo," Shelley insisting it started with an "f" because that was how it sounded and Clay gently correcting her. Shelley grudgingly accepted Clay's correction while maintaining it was unfair it was spelled this way.

"If this is not the ugliest country, then I'll be dipped," I said to no one in particular. "The only colors here are black and grey. Taking a colored picture here would be a waste of good film. What a place. Look, you can't even see any trash. Not even a single plastic bag. I don't see how anyone could live here without going stir-crazy. Or make a living, for that matter."

"Cheap land, Frankie, cheap land. A guy just might be able to make it. Raise a few head of beef, maybe a couple of sheep, sell vegetables at the Farmer's Market, work off the place during the winter—a guy just might be able to make it. Land this poor, the taxes are bound to be low. Just need to be close to water."

"Well, maybe," I said.

No one said anything for a moment, and I began thinking about Clay not taking his pills. I started to say something and then stopped, not wanting to cause an argument. But it kept eating on me because Clay had promised not to stop, and I was getting a little mad at him because he had.

"Clay, you talk to Matt about those pills?"

"Matt? Why would I talk to him about them? What does he have to do with them?"

"Well, you got your refills from him, right?"

"Matt? No, got refills through the mail. With my drug prescription plan I have under Medicare, I get a discount if I get pills through the mail, so I do. Didn't go through Matt."

"Well, you shouldn't have stopped taking them. You just shouldn't have."

Clay gave me a questioning look and then spoke in a low tone. "Give it a break, Frankie. Give it a break."

And I did, because at the moment I didn't see what else I could do. And, after all, Clay wasn't buying the boat, I was. Whatever negotiations might be necessary there'd be no reason for him to get involved. He was just along for the ride. There wouldn't be anything happening that would set him off. And maybe he was one of those that stopping taking Miazannon had no effect. We drove on in silence until Clay spoke. "Should be at the turn in less than a minute."

"Why do you say that?"

"The newspaper ad says 28 miles from the highway. Ever since we turned off the highway I've been watching the speedometer and checking my watch. Bet it's right over that rise."

And it was. Topping a small rise in the road I saw a solitary mail-box on the right-hand side, the only mail-box we had seen since we turned onto the county road.

"Ease over to the side of the road and I'll read the name on that mail-box." Clay rolled down the window and leaned his head out to get a better look. A mail-box with a hand-painted name sat on a weather-beaten post. "Does that say 'Furlings', Clay? Can you read it? I can't tell. When I called the number in the paper, I think the answering machine said 'Furlings' or something like that."

"I think so; I guess so. Can't tell for sure. It's hard to tell; the top half of the 'F' seems to be missing. Could be an 'F' or a 'P' on the mail box. How far from here? Too bad you didn't talk to him in person. Hate to drive all the way down this dirt road for nothing."

"The ad said 'about three miles.' You'd think that if you lived out here you'd know for sure. You wouldn't say 'about'. Let's give it a go. If we go more than three miles without seeing anything, we'll turn around. I called three times and never got an answer. The last time, I said that I might be out today. I didn't want to leave my number; Lucille might answer the phone if the guy called back."

"Why didn't you want Grandma talking to the boat man, Grandpa?"

"Oh, I didn't want her to be bothered. She's just not very interested in boats." Which, although not the whole truth, had sufficient truth elements that would enable me to mount a straight-face defense against a charge of not being honest with my granddaughter, in the off chance that such a charge should ever be lodged against me. Clay's rolling of his eyes told me that I better hope never to have to mount such a defense.

"Works for me," Clay said, as I turned off the pavement onto a well-worn strip of dirt that ran off in the distance, disappearing over a slight hill. Where the road was not a washboard, sharp rocks poked up through the dirt, and I hoped that Leonard had not skimped on his tires.

"Why do you suppose he's getting rid of it?" Clay asked.

"The ad didn't say. Sometimes the ad says, but this one didn't," I responded.

The road left the bench we'd been traveling on for the past five minutes and dropped into a broad valley. In the distance we could see a cluster of buildings, and just beyond the buildings was a stream bed running perpendicular to our road. A thin sliver of water could be seen in the creek bottom.

"Probably a divorce deal. You know how those divorces go. Once they split the sheets . . ."

I shot Clay a look of disapproval and his voice trailed off. Shelley's Mom and Dad separated six months ago, and she was staying with us some weekends to give them time alone, to see if they could work things out. I didn't know if they could. We were trying to make Shelley's life as easy as possible, but there was only so much we could do. Shelley would be all right, Lucille would say, kids are resilient. But I wasn't so sure.

I'd catch Shelley sitting real still, staring out the window, not playing with her dolls, not looking at any books, not doing anything. That bothered me. It was unfair; Shelley wasn't to blame for her parents' problems, yet she was caught up in their situation and had no power to change it. That just didn't seem right. I was upset with Shelley's Mom and Dad for what they were putting her through. And what they were putting me through, too, exposing me to sadness at this time of my life. By the time a guy gets to be my age, he shouldn't have to be around problems like this anymore.

"My guess is he just got tired of fishing," I said, trying to change the subject as we rolled through an open gate and into the farmstead.

It started slow. First, an old white-wall tire on the right. Then a spring-tooth harrow buried up to its axle in the dirt. An engine block, top off, four cylinders on each side exposed to the elements, leaned against a refrigerator. Soon we were in a sea of dead car bodies, pieces of farm machinery, and assorted equipment, too rusted, too torn up, or just plain too old to recognize. I spied a litter of kittens on the seat of a '65 Ford flatbed missing both doors. I started to say that the only thing lacking was a junkyard dog when a dingo raced out from under a broken-down tractor and started leaping against Clay's door, barking its fool head off. It kept flinging its body against the pickup door, and Shelley let out a scream.

"Grandpa! Grandpa, it's gonna get us, it's gonna get us!"

"I don't think so," Clay said, and he went on the offensive. Just as the dingo made another lunge at the pickup, Clay flung the door open and caught the dog square in the side of the head. Mr. dingo dog dropped like a sack of hammers. Shelley let out a shriek.

"You hurt him, Grandpa Clay! You hurt him bad! I hope he's okay."

"I hope I knocked the son-of-a-bitch into next week," muttered Clay gleefully. Shelley let out another shriek.

"Grandpa Clay, you said a bad word. You shouldn't say that word."

"Technically, Shelley, that's not a bad word," Clay said. "A 'bitch' is another name for a female dog. That dog obviously had a mother, and saying 'bitch' is just another way of saying 'mother.' I could've said 'son-of-a-mother'. I just said the same thing in another way."

"How'd ja know he was a boy dog, Grandpa Clay? It could have been a girl dog. Then it would be 'a daughter of that bad word.'"

"Looks like she's got you there, partner," I said, glancing over at Clay.

"And if you don't look out, Leonard's not going to get his pickup back in one piece!" Clay exclaimed with alarm.

I jerked my head back. A fifty-five gallon fuel barrel loomed up in front of us. The ribbon of dirt had suddenly taken a dog leg to the left. I cranked the steering wheel hard to port and then just as hard back to the right as the road ox-bowed its way through a maze of fuel barrels.

"Whoever lives here sure has a lot of stuff. What does he do with all this stuff, Grandpa?"

"Don't know," I said. "I just hope he doesn't add the dog to the price of the boat."

We stopped in front of a house, and I turned off the engine. A light rain began falling.

"And I hope that we close the deal and get out of here before the dog comes to," Clay said, opening his door and lifting Shelley to the ground. "Either that, or I hope I hit him so hard that he's got amnesia and can't remember who clobbered him."

Getting out of the pickup, I looked at the house. It was an old, one-story wooden structure that had been painted at one time but with what color was hard to tell. Most of the paint had been bleached out by the sun, and sand hurled by wind had scraped off the rest. Here and there a piece of siding was missing and tarpaper showed through. Its age was impossible to determine; growing up I had heard that during the Depression some folks just squatted on land out here and threw up shacks. At one time this house was probably better than a shack because it had store-bought windows and a real door. But a room stuck onto one side with no more than six feet of head room gave it a shack-like appearance. Smoke curled out of a rusting stove pipe, secured to the cedar shake roof with but a single strand of baling wire.

The front porch gave me a hint about the inhabitants. At one time it had been screened in, but now screen covered only one end. To the right of the front door the entire porch was filled with firewood stacked clear to the ceiling. To the left of the door sat a couch with no center cushion, and next to it was a refrigerator without a door. On the top shelf of the refrigerator I could see more than a dozen end wrenches, laid out from left to right in a descending order of lengths. Below the wrenches, on the next shelf down, were several screwdrivers arranged not only by size, but also by type. My tool bench had never looked so organized. I was curious about why a guy would have tools on his front porch and not where he would be working, like in his shop. Then I saw a "For Sale" sign, hand-written, duct-taped to the refrigerator above the wrenches. There was a sign by the screwdrivers as well.

The house had an odd appearance, and I couldn't figure why until I zeroed in on the posts supporting the roof of the porch. There were six of them, all off plumb. And the peculiar thing about these posts was that they were all off plumb by what appeared to be exactly the same amount. The uniformity of this lean caused me to think the tilt was intentional, although I could perceive no reason why that would be so. While examining the orientation of the posts, the roof of the porch caught my eye. The tilting of the posts, or whatever made the posts tilt in the first place, had caused the roof to separate from the house. The eastern end of the roof, the direction in which the posts were tilting, now extended beyond the side of the house a good two feet. The whole effect created the impression that the roof of the porch, accompanied by the posts, had decided to pack and leave, while the rest of the house had resolutely reached the opposite conclusion, choosing to remain firmly rooted where it was. The separation looked old, the break was badly weathered, and I wondered how somebody could let their place go like this. I was thinking that whoever lived here must have just given up when I heard a door open and a voice from the inside.

"I'll be right outside here, honey," I heard a man say, and then he stepped out the front door and onto the edge of the porch.

Chapter 9
Will and Annie

He was as modest-looking as the house. The baseball hat perched on his head bore the logo of a feed co-op that went bust five years ago, and the bill of his hat was beginning to separate from the rest of the cap. Numerous grease spots dotted the front of his army surplus coat and thin streaks of white paint ran down both sleeves. Multiple patches covered a faded pair of blue jeans. His boots were well worn but I recognized the brand; they were quality boots. As for the man himself, I'd put him at around fifty—and a hard fifty at that. And small, maybe no more than 5'4", but it was difficult to say for sure. A mass of wavy, jet-black hair sticking out a good three inches from underneath his hat made his exact height difficult to peg.

In his right hand the man held a white porcelain coffee cup from which wisps of steam rose. With his left, he partially unzipped his coat and from a shirt pocket took out a beige-colored cloth bag and a small flat container. I watched his manipulation of these items intently, recognizing them instantly from a distant past. Using only the first finger of his left hand, he opened the top of the bag and dumped some tobacco onto a piece of paper he'd removed from the flat container. Without spilling any tobacco, the man rolled a perfect cigarette. He put it in his mouth and, with a match struck off his thumbnail, lit it. At no time during this entire operation did the coffee cup leave the man's right hand. It had been at least fifty years since I'd seen anyone roll their own, using tobacco, so observing an expert at it brought back pleasant memories. For some reason I could not quite articulate, I felt comforted to see a practice from my childhood still alive.

The man exhaled a large cloud of smoke and finally looked at us, his face bearing a quizzical expression. I'm guessing it's not every day two guys on the wrong side of 65 and a 7-year-old girl show up on his doorstep.

"The boat," I said. "We came about the boat. I called yesterday and said we might be coming out today to look at it. I left a message on your answering machine."

The man shifted his weight and zipped up his coat against the cold. Jamming both hands into his coat pockets, the man took another drag on the cigarette hanging from his lower lip. Then he spoke, exhaling as he did. "The price is set; I'm not gonna lower it. It's a fair price, everything considered. The trailer's included."

"She's probably not licensed, is she?" It was more of an accusation from Clay than a question.

"I don't take her much on the road and, anyway, the sheriff don't come around here hardly never, so I don't see no need to buy any license. Money don't grow on trees around here."

I looked around. Except for a couple of scrawny aspen trees down by the creek, there weren't any trees at all. And it didn't look like anything grew around here if you didn't count the occasional sagebrush. Calling the place barren and desolate might be too favorable a description. Godforsaken would be closer to home. I was getting depressed just being here.

"How do we know the motor even works? You can't expect us to take your word for it; we've got to see it." This was Clay's opening negotiating gambit.

The guy stood up ramrod straight and glared at Clay.

"This fall, the last time I used it, I ran all of the gas out of the motor; ran it all out and then pulled on the starter cord at least a dozen times to make sure that there weren't no gas left in her to gum up the plugs. Then I squirted sewing machine oil into each chamber and put the plugs back in. I drained all of the water out of her, too, so she wouldn't freeze up during the winter. What do you think I am, some guy who don't know how take care of his equipment?"

"I look around here at all of this stuff, most of which I bet doesn't run, and I don't know. I just don't know what we'd be getting into. We might be buying a pig in a poke."

"You feel that way, maybe you should just get right back in that pickup of yours and turn around." The man stepped off the porch.

"We didn't come all the way out here just to turn around. We're going to take a look at that boat." A hard edge had crept into Clay's voice, and he took a step away from the pickup toward the porch.

I was the one putting up the money; Clay was just along for the ride, maybe to give me a hand hefting stuff around if I needed it. But that was it. It wasn't his deal, so where did he get off doing the negotiating? He was gonna mess the whole thing up, and then we would have wasted the entire day driving out here, to say nothing about spending money on the boat hitches and the running lights.

I was about to jump in before everything went sideways when Shelley piped up. "Grandpa, I'm cold. Can I go inside?"

With all the sparks flying around, I had temporarily forgotten about Shelley.

The man's body relaxed, and he held out his hand toward Shelley.

"Sure, come on in. We've got a big fire going, and I'll see if I can find some hot chocolate for you." He stepped back to the door and opened it up for Shelley. Shelley looked up at me, questioning.

"I think that a cup of hot chocolate is a good idea," I said.

"Yeah, and she can keep my wife company while we do our business. When I got your phone call, I put the motor in a barrel of water and tried to start it. It started on the second pull. Ran fine for three minutes, and then I shut her off. It's still in that barrel, so we can test it if you like. Come on in out of this cold while I make some cocoa."

The man pinched off the burning end of his cigarette and stomped on the ember as it hit the ground. He put the rest of the cigarette in a square tin he'd taken out of a coat pocket and motioned us all in with a hand. "I don't smoke inside no more," he said as I walked inside with Shelley, "and oh, by the way, I'm Will."

Clay stood on the porch, hesitating as if he weren't sure the invitation included him, but Will waved again and Clay stepped over the threshold. Standing inside the house, I introduced myself and Clay and we shook hands all around. In the warmth of the room, the chilly atmosphere was gone. While Will was finding the cocoa and running water into a teapot, I looked around the room we had just entered.

There was a table with two mismatched chairs, a refrigerator that must have been forty years old, a large sink, and a wood stove that was the only visible source of heat. In the center of the ceiling a solitary light bulb hung from a twisted cord. The walls were bare except for a year-old calendar and a black-and-white photograph of a man and woman in wedding clothes. The man in the photo looked like a young Will.

In the corner of the room, where the light wasn't very good, a fake leather recliner faced an old sofa. Half sitting, half lying on the sofa with a quilt pulled up to her neck was a thin woman, tissue-paper white. She spoke in a weak, raspy voice. "I've got the cancer bad, really bad." Her tone was apologetic, as if it was inhospitable for her to be so sick.

"I carry her from the bed to the couch, even to the toilet. Most days now she's so weak I have to feed her. She can't even lift a spoon. But that don't matter now."

I turned to look at Will. Light from one of the two windows in the room fell on his face. Anger flashed across it as he spoke again.

"Annie was doing okay when we had insurance. Then the premium went up almost twenty-five percent, and we didn't have the cash. Just didn't have her. We tried to get help from the state, but she wasn't old enough, and they said we weren't poor enough. Had too much property to qualify. Too much property! Guess they never heard of being 'dirt poor.' No one is gonna buy this place, no matter how low we set the price. What with the price of fertilizer and all, wheat don't pay for itself, and the cattle market is in the ash-can. I'm selling off stuff now just to pay the lights and put some food on the table. Got this place from her folks, darn near twenty years ago now, and worked just about every day since. Can't get ahead, just can't. This place grinds a guy down, down to practically nothing."

He got a catch in his throat, paused a moment, and then went on. His voice lost its anger, replaced by a softness.

"The pain was the thing. Couldn't get no drugs from town. Didn't have cash, and no one would give me credit. Don't blame 'em none for that, though. But we figured out a way around that problem, didn't we, sweetie?" Will smiled at his wife, and she smiled weakly back.

He started to go on, then caught himself, like he didn't want to tell strangers some secret. I tried to think of something to say, something on the bright side, but there wasn't any bright side to this. So we all stood there in an awkward silence.

"Hey, the water's boiling," Shelley said. For the second time today I had almost forgotten about her. This time it was because of Will's story.

"Oh yeah, you're right," Will said. "It looks like it's about ready." He took a coffee cup and spoon out of a dish rack and got a large can of powdered cocoa out of a cupboard. Scooping two heaping spoonfuls of cocoa into the cup, Will poured boiling water in, stirred it probably longer than necessary, and then handed the cup to Shelley.

"I don't like my cocoa real hot. Sometimes I put an ice cube in it, to cool it down fast so I can drink it right away and not have to wait. Jennifer showed me how to do that. She's my best friend. You got any ice cubes?" Shelley asked.

Will looked embarrassed.

"Our refrigerator is kinda on the fritz. Haven't had any ice for quite a while."

Shelley must have sensed his embarrassment. "Oh, that's okay. I can blow on it. That's what we do when we don't have any ice cubes."

"Shelley, why don't you stay in here and drink your cocoa while Clay and Will and I go look at the boat," I said.

"Yeah," Will said. "Like I said outside, you can keep Annie company. We don't hardly get nobody out here. In fact, about the only visitor we do get is the meter reader. He was here last week, and we won't see him again for another two months. You grab a seat over there next to Annie and have a nice chat with her, tell her what you've been doing today. She'd like that. We'll be looking at the boat. It's out back in the barn."

Without any hesitation, as if she'd known Annie all her life, Shelley walked over to the recliner and sat down. She wiggled her way into the back of the chair and then, satisfied with her position, blew across her cocoa.

Will was at the door with his hand on the knob. He was about to turn it when he saw I wasn't moving toward him. I was watching Shelley, making sure she was settling in okay with a stranger, with someone who was dying. Annie looked up at Shelley expectantly.

Shelley leaned forward and began. "Well, today, this morning I got up at 6:13. No, that was yesterday. Today I got up at 6:17. You know what I think is funny? The numbers after lunch are smaller than the numbers before lunch, on the clock. That doesn't seem right to me. The day is older in the afternoon than in the morning, and the numbers in the afternoon should be bigger, bigger than in the morning. Because older kids have more numbers than younger kids. But that's not the way it works, and I don't know why. I think I'll ask my Grandpa. No, no, I'm gonna ask Grandpa Clay. He knows about numbers, he's a 'counten.'"

I looked over at Clay. He was watching Shelley, too, smiling. So was Will, standing at the door with his hand still on the knob.

"Well, anyways," Shelley said, continuing the description of her day. "After I got up, I made my bed. Grandma says you should always make your bed as soon as you get up because that way it will be ready when you go to sleep at night. Then I put Charlotte and Betty on the pillows. Charlotte and Betty are my two dolls. I have other dolls at home, but Mommy says I can only bring two to Grandma's and Grandpa's. I wanted to go downstairs because I got hungry, but I can't be in the kitchen unless there is an adult there. That's the rule. But I heard Grandpa making coffee, so I knew it was okay. I took Charlotte to eat breakfast with me this morning because it was her turn today. I can only take one doll with me downstairs because I have to hold on to the railing with the other hand when I'm on the stairs because young children have to hold on to the railing when they're on the stairs. But I heard Grandma tell Grandpa he had to hold on to the railing when he goes downstairs, so maybe that's the rule for grown-ups, too."

Clay chuckled at the last remark, breaking the mesmerizing spell of Shelley's monologue.

"Hey, Grandpa, give me your arm and I'll help you to the door," Clay said, chuckling again and sliding his arm through mine. Arm in arm, we walked outside.

"And I thought Lucille was the only person who could carry on both ends of a conversation all by herself. Guess I was wrong about that; it looks like Lucille passed that gene on to your granddaughter." Clay was still smirking as we stepped off the porch together.

We rounded the back of the house and headed toward a barn about a hundred feet away. The area between the house and the barn was as cluttered with junk as the drive into the house. We followed Will as he navigated his way through an array of discarded machinery.

"Hey, get a look at that. The last time I saw a washing machine that old, it was sitting on my grandmother's back porch."

I turned to where Clay was looking. An old-fashioned washing machine, one with rollers, leaned up against a well that appeared to be abandoned. Most of the white paint was chipped off. Further past the well, on a small rise about fifty feet from us, I noticed a fresh pile of dirt.

Just to have some conversation as we walked, I made a comment about the dirt. "Looks like you're getting ready to bury some of this dead machinery up there," I said, pointing to the mound of dirt.

As the words were leaving my mouth, I tried to snatch them back. But I couldn't.

Will stopped moving and turned to face the rise. He cleared his throat twice and then spoke. "She's not gonna last the week, Annie isn't. I called up the doctor yesterday and told him what was going on with her and that's what he said. Said all I could do was make her comfortable. No reason to bring her in to the hospital. There was nothing they could do for her. Annie hasn't been able to eat for the last three days, and yesterday, in the whole day, I could barely get one glass of water down her. I'm gonna bury her right over there," Will said, indicating with his hand to the fresh pile of dirt I had pointed out.

"She picked out her spot last month," he continued, "when she was still able to get around some. I dug her grave with her watching. Didn't want to dig it, but she insisted. Said we had to be sensible about it. Said it was something we could do together, me digging and her giving encouragement and advice every now and then. When it got deeper, she wanted to see the whole thing, so I got her right over to the edge, so she could look clear down to the bottom. She watched me finish it off, square off the corners for the box. When I climbed out, she was looking down into it. Said it looked kinda empty. I said, 'What about some flowers?' She said, 'Where you're gonna get flowers this time of year? This late in the fall, everything's dead.' 'I know a spot,' I said. 'Down by the creek. I'll be right back.' I wasn't sure I could find any, but there's a place down by the creek that's out of the wind and gets sun most of the day. I looked there and, sure enough, there were a dozen or so yellow wild roses still in bloom. I took out my jackknife, cut 'em off, and brought them back to her, lying there next to her grave. I helped her to her feet, and she grabbed my hand, the one holding those roses. We stood there for a moment, on the edge, looking at each other, holding on to those roses together. Then she said, 'You gotta let go, Will. You gotta let go.' And we threw 'em in."

He was silent for a moment. I looked at him, thinking he was probably a little embarrassed about sharing something so private with strangers. But it wasn't embarrassment I saw on his face, it was pride. And strangely enough, I felt a little pride for him, too, seeing a guy who had figured out all on his own how to get through a really tough spot. And it seemed a good way, too, just right for the circumstances, just about perfect. I wanted to tell him that, to congratulate him on coming up with what he had done, but I couldn't quite put the words "grave" and "congratulations" in the same sentence. I looked over at Clay to see if he was coming up with something. He wasn't; he was just staring down at the ground, wiggling his ears.

Will went on.

"All the way back to the house, carrying her, I cried. Bawled my eyes out. Kept on crying even after I laid her down on the sofa. When I finally stopped, we had a long talk, about how we'd had a good life together and things like that. Had a few laughs, too. Went to bed feeling a little better, and I'm okay with it now. I know it will be a shock when it happens, but I'm ready for it now, and that feels better, a lot better. She's picked out the dress she wants to wear and the things she wants me to say. It'll be just the two of us. We don't have any kin or kids or any close friends anymore. But we're used to being by ourselves, so that's okay, too. I'll be there for her at the end, to lay her in the grave, and her knowing that I'll be there at the end has brought her real peace. I see that now, every time I look at her. And that helps me, too, a lot."

We reached the barn, and Will slid the door open.

Chapter 10
The Boat

Stepping inside, I was surprised how light it was. There were only a couple of small windows, and those were mostly obscured with dirt and dust. I looked around to see where the light was coming from. Over against one wall, under a tent-like structure made out of thick, clear plastic, I could see a ten-foot row of lights above a table. Most of the lights were fluorescent, but a couple glowed red.

"She's over here," Will said, hitting a light switch that illuminated the interior of the barn.

I expected to see a boat covered with a layer of dust, seat cushions eaten away by mice, and the whole thing littered with rodent droppings. Instead, Will had wrapped the boat in a couple of blue tarps and secured the tarps with rope and bungee cords. It took him almost two minutes to untie and unwrap everything. It was immaculate, like it had just come off the showroom floor. Clay and I walked around it, neither one of us wanting to say anything about the steal we were getting for fear Will might jack up the price.

"The engine runs good. Here, I'll show you." Will headed toward one side of the barn where I could see a 10-horse Johnson outboard sitting in a fifty-five gallon barrel of water. I followed him. I didn't see what Clay was doing.

Will primed the engine, grabbed the starter rope, and gave it two quick pulls. The engine started on the second pull. He let it idle for a minute and turned the handle, giving the engine more gas. It roared. Will let it run on high for another minute and then throttled it back down to let it idle before shutting it off. The engine ran great; we were getting a great deal.

"She's only got about fifteen hours on it. We bought it to go fishing on Rose Lake. It's only about twenty minutes from here on a good back road. Has real nice-size native cutthroat. Annie really likes to fish; we got it more for her than me. But she can't do it anymore. Last time we went, got down to the boat ramp, but didn't even launch the boat. Said she didn't have the strength even to get out of the car. She was right. I had to carry her into the house when we got back home. That was in September. Hadn't even had the boat but a year."

That struck me as odd, a couple as poor as Will and Annie coming up with enough cash to buy a new boat and motor. Will must have read my thoughts.

"I know what you're thinking, how could we afford to buy this boat; where'd we get the money? A year ago in the fall, we sold off the rest of the cattle. We didn't have many head left, fifteen maybe, in all. We didn't have enough hay put up for even that small number, rain just didn't come at the right time, and of course we couldn't afford to buy hay for the winter. We knew most wouldn't make it to spring with what little hay we had, and those that did wouldn't be worth a darn, so we took 'em all to the auction and sold the lot. I was thinking we'd use the money to get some of our equipment up and running, or maybe fix the porch roof where I hit it with the bucket of the front-end loader rounding the corner of the house. But Annie talked me into buying the boat. Saw an ad in the paper that the store was selling a boat cheap. She said we never did anything for ourselves, just poured everything we made back into the place. Said we should spend some of the money on ourselves; we were getting old, and you never knew what might happen. She remembered the good times she had fishing with her dad growing up here and thought the both of us would enjoy it. Turns out she was right on both scores. This spring and early summer we went fishing a lot and had a great time, even when we didn't catch any fish. And then Annie got the cancer. The fifteenth of July, we found that out."

Will paused for a moment, and then went on.

"This fall, when I put the boat away after our last fishing trip, I cleaned it all up. Washed off the mud and the slime, polished the hull, even took the vacuum to the inside. I don't know why, really. I guess I did it for her, for Annie. It was more her boat than mine. I wanted to do something for her, so I got her boat in good shape. I know it sounds kinda funny saying it, but I thought maybe if I took care of her boat good, her cancer would stop spreading. But it didn't; it didn't slow down at all."

Will's voice trailed off at the end. I looked at Will, thinking he would be embarrassed by telling me how he tried to stop Annie's cancer. He wasn't embarrassed; he looked exhausted, drained of energy by the finality of his wife's illness.

Our uncomfortable silence was broken by Clay. "Hey, you got marijuana growing in here. What's going on here?"

Will and I looked up. Clay had opened up one end of the plastic tent and was peering inside. Will got a worried look on his face.

"It's for Annie's cancer. I heard that marijuana helps with the pain, so in the fall I bought a little bit from a guy in town and Annie smoked it. It helped her, a lot. I couldn't afford to buy any more, so I decided to grow my own. Got some plants real cheap, took lights from the chicken coop, and rigged up this little greenhouse. It's the only thing that stops the pain."

"I don't care what's it for. It's illegal. You can't have these in here." Clay was now inside the tent, and I could see through the plastic he was jerking plants up. *Why is Clay doing that?* I thought. I never knew him to be against marijuana, or for it, for that matter. The subject just never came up after our teenage years when we both tried it. But there he was, pulling up marijuana plants like a man possessed.

"Hey, what are you doing in there? Stop that!"

Will ran over to the greenhouse and darted inside. I could see that he was trying to get between Clay and the plants. Suddenly I got scared, really really scared.

Will shoved Clay away from the plants, toward the door of the greenhouse. Clay must have tripped over something because he tumbled out the door, stumbling backwards a couple of feet until falling down on six inches of straw that covered that area of the barn floor. When he came up, he had an axe handle in both hands, holding it like a baseball bat.

"Clay, no!" I yelled.

Will was now just outside the greenhouse door. He held up his left hand to ward off the blow, but the axe handle caught him right on the left cheek bone, making a sickening, crunching sound.

"Grandpa Clay!"

I turned to look. I saw Shelley standing in the doorway of the barn, saw her white porcelain coffee cup slipping from her hand, cocoa spilling over the brim, racing the cup to the concrete floor, the cup shattering in pieces, cocoa splashing up Shelley's legs. The cocoa must have been hot because she gave out a little cry.

"The lady fell asleep, and I got a little scared all by myself, so I was looking for you guys." Shelley's eyes grew wide as she clasped both her hands over her mouth and looked past me. I looked back to where Shelley was looking.

Will was down on his right knee, his left arm held up in front of his face; he was using his left leg to push himself away from Clay. One side of Will's face was all caved in, splinters of bone poking through the skin. Clay raised the axe handle over his head.

"Clay, are you nuts? What do you think you're doing?"

He turned toward me. I've heard the phrase *crazed expression* and thought I knew what it meant. I didn't. Looking into Clay's face was like looking into the soul of the devil. The absolute evil in his eyes paralyzed me with fear.

Will used this momentary distraction to try to escape from Clay, scooting away from him on his knees. His luck ran out when he reached the wall of the barn. Clay took two steps and was on top Will, the axe handle high over his head. He brought it down, but he was too close to wall, and the axe handle bounced off the wall with a loud *bang*, cracking a board. Clay let out a yelp of pain as the axe handle dropped onto Will's back and then onto the floor. Methodically, Clay picked up the axe handle with his right hand only and took one step back, his left arm hanging limp at his side.

Now using only his right hand, Clay brought the handle down on Will's head. Will tried to stand up. I thought that he was going to make it, but just as he was trying to straighten up, he lost his balance, slumping to the ground on his knees with his head falling to the floor, emitting a weak whimper. Clay beat on Will's head with a steady rhythm; I couldn't tell how many times, could have been five, could have just as easily been fifteen. Will completely stopped moving after the first two or three blows, but Clay didn't. It was like he was pounding a nail in, and he really wanted to drive it home. At the end, his face was beet-red, glowing with sweat; his breath was coming in rasping gasps. He staggered over to a block of wood and almost slipped off it as he clumsily sat down.

I looked at Clay, wondering what was going to happen next. It took him at least two minutes before his breathing evened out. Slowly his expression changed, gradually losing any trace of evil, and he let go of the axe handle. It barely made a sound landing on the hay scattered on the barn floor. A good three minutes passed; then he stood up and walked over to where Will was. With his good hand Clay grabbed the cuff of one of Will's pant legs and started dragging him toward the barn door. He had to detour around Shelley, who had not moved from the doorway. I rushed over and picked her up. Her body was shaking like she was sobbing, but no noise was coming out. Holding her tightly, we sat down on a hay bale just inside the barn door. I was rocking her gently when Clay yelled out.

"Frankie, I need you out here."

I didn't say anything, just continued rocking Shelley.

"Frankie, I can't do it myself; I need you. C'mon, get out here."

I set Shelley down on the hay bale and looked out the barn door. Clay was standing next to the well, rubbing his left shoulder, grimacing in pain. Will was lying at his feet in a heap. The lid was off the well.

"I jammed up my shoulder. Must have done it when I hit the wall. Don't have a bit of strength in my arm. Can't get him over the edge. He's way too heavy. Grab a leg here and help me."

"He might not be dead, Clay. We should try to get some help for him."

"He's dead, Frankie—deader than a stone. Get over here and give me a hand with him. Can't just leave him here out in the open. Someone might find him. Get over here."

I stepped back inside the barn to see how Shelley was doing. Her eyes were closed, and she had wrapped her arms around her. I was debating whether it was all right to leave her alone for a second when Clay gave out another shout for help. I turned away from Shelley and walked out of the barn toward the well, not sure what I was going to do. Clay yelled at me to hurry up, and I broke into a jog.

He was bent down with both hands on one of Will's legs. I could tell by the way his left hand was on the leg that he had no strength in that side.

"Here, grab his other leg."

I hesitated. How many cases had I had, when I was a young attorney just starting out doing criminal cases as a public defender, where my guy had not committed the main crime involved but had done something minor, something that helped the instigator in some modest way? Caught up in the heat of the moment, the adrenaline-charged, frenzied atmosphere inherent in the commission of a crime apparently rendered these peripheral actors susceptible to pleas for assistance. More than once as they were led away to prison I found myself thinking, they just had to walk away; that's all they had to do, just walk away. And that's what I was thinking as I looked down at Will's limp body, until Clay spoke sharply to me.

"Hey, you need to grab his leg. We can't leave him out here. We need to get him out of sight. No one will find him if we dump him down there. We'll be okay once he's down there."

It might have been Clay's use of the plural "we," implying I was already involved; we were in this together. Or maybe it was 60 years of relying on his judgment. Or maybe it was simply because my best friend was in a jam and needed my help, and that's what best friends do, they help out.

I looked all around in every direction. No witnesses, no one would know. Will wasn't going to get any deader. I bent down and grabbed a leg, and we humped him over the edge. He crashed to the bottom.

I stared down into the well; it was deep—forty, maybe fifty feet down. And dark, but I could make out Will, or at least his legs up to his waist. The rest of him was in the shadows. I was still looking down at Will when I heard the truck honk, first once and then three times in rapid succession. I looked up from the well, and Clay was not there. He left without me realizing it, and was now in the pickup. The horn honked again. I looked back at the barn. Shelley was peering around the corner of the doorway; the knuckles of both thumbs were in her mouth. She hadn't done that since she was three. I carried her to the pickup.

Clay was seated in the passenger side, looking way off in the distance, but I don't think he was seeing anything, the way his eyes looked. I opened the driver's-side door and slid Shelley under the steering wheel.

I strapped Shelley in the seatbelt, climbed in, and strapped myself in. I put my arm around Shelley, pulling her as close to me as possible. Clay looked over to me and then looked back without saying a word. On the way out to the county road, I didn't see a single animal, not a dog, not a cat, not even a bird. Nothing was moving, not even the weeds; it was dead calm. Shelley was asleep by the time we hit the blacktop.

We'd been on the county road about fifteen minutes when I said, "This is not like Mollie, Clay. This is different."

Clay just kept looking straight ahead, not saying a word, but his jaw was clenched so tight the veins in his neck bulged like a swollen river.

I thought maybe he hadn't heard me, so I repeated myself. "Clay, this is a person, a human being. It's different."

"Not to me, it isn't; no difference to me, Frankie, no difference at all."

That was the extent of the conversation, the entire hour and half drive back to town. I had a lot of time to think on the way, and I did. I played over the scene in the barn and the scene at the well over and over and over, until with the familiarity caused by repetition the shock pretty much dissipated. That's when I was able to feel some anger—anger at Clay for talking me into helping him, and anger at myself for agreeing to help him. But by the time we hit the edge of town that, too, wore off. I never could seem to stay mad at Clay very long; that was part and parcel of a sixty-year friendship. Turning into his street I was beginning to feel sad for him; given his mental condition I couldn't see he had much to look forward to for the rest of his life. As for me, I tried telling myself I had nothing to worry about; no one had seen me help Clay.

I pulled up in front of Clay's house, and he was out of the pickup before we came to a complete stop, leaving the door open. I reached over the still-sleeping Shelley and pulled the door closed. Clay walked up the front steps to his porch, not looking back. As I drove out of his driveway, I wondered what he was thinking. Heading home, I was struck by the feeling that there was something odd about our drive into town, like there was something that should have been there but wasn't. We were a block away from home when it hit me. It was his ears. All the way back, not once did Clay's ears move, not a millimeter. He wasn't thinking at all what he had done out there in the country; it didn't concern him a bit.

When I rolled into my driveway the house was dark, which meant that Lucille wasn't home. I was glad for that because right then I didn't want to face her, to answer her innocent question, "So how was your day?" Entering the house, I realized I hadn't eaten all day, not lunch, not dinner. Generally when I miss a meal I get so hungry I could eat the hindquarters off a road-killed cat. But this evening I had no appetite.

I carried Shelley, still sleeping, up to the bedroom she used when she stayed with us, undressed her, and put her in her favorite pj's, the white ones with cute blue bunnies hopping around. As I tucked her in, I wondered what she would be dreaming. I found out the next morning when she came down for breakfast, still in her pj's and carrying a giraffe, her favorite stuffed animal.

Chapter 11
Shelley

"Grandpa, can I ask you a question?"

I was seated at the breakfast bar, working on my first cup of coffee. I looked at her standing there, in the doorway to the kitchen, my mind spinning, trying to come up with an answer to the question I knew was coming.

I blinked a couple of times and then answered her. "Sure, honey, ask away."

"Do outhouses stink?"

I spit out the coffee I was holding in my mouth, covering most of the countertop. That was not the question I was expecting.

"Jennifer says they stink so bad I won't be able to use them. That's what her brother told her when he went to Science Camp last year. If they stink, I don't want to go to camp. Mommy says Jennifer has a cold and isn't going to camp, but I think she's not going because outhouses stink."

Shelley and her mother were headed for a week-long science camp at a lake about two hours away. I was expecting my daughter to show up around 10:00 this morning to pick up Shelley and head for camp.

I was explaining to Shelley the chemistry of the effect of lye on outhouses and assuring her that her outhouse would be bearable, when the phone rang. It was Clay.

"Frankie, we need to talk. Can you come over here, right away?"

I heard Lucille rustling around upstairs and knew she would be down in a moment. Shelley would be fine by herself until then; she was peeling a banana, and that would occupy her attention until her grandmother arrived.

"Sure, Clay. Let me grab a second cup of coffee, and I'll head your way."

"Forget the coffee. I've got some here. Just get over here."

I said okay and hung up.

I put on my hat and coat and looked for a travel mug to put coffee in for the drive over to Clay's. Nothing could be so important that it would require me to wait five minutes for my second cup of coffee. I was filling the mug when Shelley spoke again. This time her question was not about outhouses.

"Grandpa, I had a dream last night about Grandpa Clay hitting some man with a stick, real hard. The man fell down and couldn't get up. But he wouldn't do that, would he?" She had finished peeling the banana and was closely inspecting it for any sign of brown spots. Shelley would not eat a banana unless it was perfectly white. The one in her hand must have passed the test because she bit off a piece that filled her mouth.

"Nah, Grandpa Clay wouldn't do that. I think maybe you've been watching a little too much TV."

Yeah, you're probably right. Momma says there's way too much violence on TV."

"Your mom's right."

I hesitated before asking the next question. They say when you're cross-examining a witness, never ask a question if you don't already know the answer. But I had to know the answer to this question. "Shelley, what happened in your dream after the man fell down?"

"I don't know. I woke up. Grandma was snoring real loud and she woke me up. Nothing happened to him; it was just a dream."

"Yeah, it was just a dream," I repeated. "Say, you'll probably be gone by the time I get back from Clay's, so have a great time at camp this week and say hello to your mom for me. And don't pay any attention to what Jennifer says, okay? She doesn't know what she's talking about."

"Okay, Grandpa," Shelley said. At least that's what I think she said; it was hard to tell for sure with her mouth full of banana. Getting into the pickup I spotted a piece of white paper on the floorboard. The number "9" was scrawled on it. Lucille's needle! I had forgotten all about it yesterday. Good thing I was asleep when she got home last night, and that I got out the door this morning before she came downstairs. I put the piece of paper on the seat. I could pick up Lucille's needle after having coffee with Clay; she would never know the difference.

I walked in Clay's back door without knocking and saw him sitting at the kitchen table with a stack of papers in front of him.

There's a checkerboard pattern on Clay's kitchen table, and he was pushing the stack around on the table, his hands in non-stop motion. He was still careful with his left arm, but I could see it was working better than yesterday. At first I couldn't tell what he was doing. Then I saw. Clay was trying to line up the stack of papers with the checkerboard lines on the table, trying to get the top and bottom of the stack aligned with the lines running horizontally, and both sides of the stack lined up with the lines running vertically. But it wasn't working for him.

He would get the top lined up perfectly, and then get the left side lined up. But when he tried to line up the bottom of the stack, he would move the top of the stack off the line it was on, and when he got the right side lined up, the left side would move off its line. It was like trying to eat soup with a fork; it just wasn't going to happen. The grid lines on the table were too far apart to match up with the stack. Clay couldn't see that; he just kept working on the stack, moving it in a counter-clockwise direction to get first the top lined up, then the left, then the bottom, then the right, round and round, moving at the same constant speed. He didn't seem to be frustrated or upset he couldn't get it right; he just pursed his lips and kept moving the stack. I sat down opposite him and watched him for another moment, and then I couldn't stand it anymore. I slapped my hand down on the stack, and Clay's hands stopped moving.

He looked up at me, a faraway look in his eyes. He blinked a couple of times and then spoke. "Oh, Frankie, how come you're here?"

"What've you got there?" I said, pointing to the stack of papers. Now that they had stopped moving I could make out the words *Fortieth Year Annual Marine Reunion*.

"I'm thinking of going, Frankie. Haven't gone before, and may not be around for the next one. It's my old Marine Regiment's annual reunion. It would be good to see some of the guys, those that are still around."

He continued, "I can catch the bus from Middleton to get to Florida from there, but I'm worried about leaving my car at the bus station while I'm at the reunion. No telling what might happen to it. Some teenager may just decide to tag it or let the air out of the tires, just for fun. And I need to get someone to feed Mollie."

I looked up from the papers. Now Clay seemed as normal as ever, except he'd completely forgotten that Mollie was dead.

Clay took a sip of tea and then continued talking. "What'd she say about me, last night or this morning? What's she saying?"

"Who?" I asked.

"What do you mean, who? You know who I'm talking about. Shelley. What's she saying about me?"

I hesitated for a moment, trying to think of just the right way to answer, but that was a mistake. Clay homed right in on my uncertainty.

"She's talking about me, isn't she? I knew it, I just knew it. Tell me what's she saying."

I hesitated again. Again, a big mistake.

"Frank, you tell me. You tell me right now, you hear!" The look in Clay's eyes terrified me—terrified me because it was so frightening and double terrified me because I'd never before seen this expression on his face, not in the sixty-plus years I'd known him. It wasn't Clay looking at me across the kitchen table; it was a stranger.

"It was just a dream, Clay. Shelley just had a dream. Didn't mean anything, nothing at all."

"I knew it. I just knew it. I'm gonna have to take care of her."

"Take care of Shelley—what are you talking about?"

"Put her away, like the guy."

I shot to my feet like I'd been jabbed by a cattle prod, knocking over my chair in the process. Leaning over the table toward him, I started a couple of sentences, but my words, propelled by shock and fear for Shelley, kept tripping over each other, making no sense.

I took a deep breath and settled on a single word. "Why?"

"She's gonna tell someone I killed the guy. She can't help it; she's just a kid, and kids tell people about stuff like that all the time. It'll get back to the cops in no time, and they'll haul me up in front of Hanging Harry. He's just looking for someone like me to hammer, after he let that banker's son off with just community service and two days later the kid killed someone, driving drunk again. Harry's up for re-election next year, and a couple of lawyers are already gunning for his spot. There won't be any community service for me; they'll be looking to stick a needle in me in no time," Clay said, pantomiming someone putting a hypodermic needle in his forearm.

I was stunned by what I'd just heard, not only by what Clay had said, but maybe more so by the matter-of-fact way he spoke. I tried to convince myself I hadn't heard him right, because this wasn't like my Clay. Then I thought about Will, and the teenager, and Mollie. My Clay had committed those acts, too. And that's when I finally saw clearly the effect of Clay's change, the consequences of his detachment from reality. Mollie was an animal, not a human. Will was a stranger, someone Clay had known for less than an hour, not enough time for a bond to form between them. But Shelley, Clay did have a bond with her, and that should have been a barrier to him harming her. But that barrier now was gone, eroded away by this particular decay in his mental faculties. My legs felt weak and started to tremble. I reached for the back of the chair and set it up right. I hit only half the seat sitting down, staring at Clay across the table from me.

He was back to trying to line up the stack of papers with the lines on the table, his lips pursed as if he was concentrating as hard as he could. About every third trip around the circle with the papers he would stop to take a drink of his tea. I watched him for a while, not saying anything, trying to get my thoughts under control, to first process the realization my old Clay was not coming back, and then what he was saying about Shelley. Each prospect was so unnatural, so foreign, that they would disintegrate before I could wrap my arms around them. Maybe it was because I couldn't, or didn't want to, acknowledge what I was seeing. My mind was spinning so rapidly I felt unsteady and with both hands grabbed the edge of the kitchen table to anchor myself.

It did not help matters, he was so calm, so nonchalant. To me, this was a monumental act he was proposing, a life-changing event for Shelley of course, but for him, too. But he was just so matter-of-fact about it, and now that got under my skin. I was on the verge of screaming at him when he stopped moving the stack of papers and looked up at me.

"Clay, listen to what you are saying," I blurted out, my voice barely under control. "You want to kill someone. And not just anybody, but Shelley. She's like a granddaughter to you; you've said so lots of time yourself. You love Shelley, and Shelley loves you. I'm sure there's some way we can take care of this, if it should ever get back to the cops." I instantly regretted saying the last, its tone of desperation conveying my lack of conviction in its validity.

For a moment, though, I thought I had got to him, from the reaction in his eyes when I said Shelley loved him. Clay hesitated for a moment, the stack of papers not moving. Then he shrugged his shoulders.

"Frankie, my boy, you're not that good of an attorney. Don't think anyone is. Got to be, it's got to be. Can't see any way around it. I didn't work all those years to spend my retirement looking out of bars, waiting for my death-penalty appeals to run out." It was the tone of his voice that got to me. Not angry or frightening or threatening. It was as if the consequences of his actions would be minor, insignificant. The thought struck me that Clay was being arrogant, placing more value on the few years he had remaining than all the years Shelley had left. Or maybe he was just selfless. My respect for Clay dropped a couple of notches, as did my fondness for him.

"She's not in town, Clay. Shelley's spending the week at High Up, the science camp they run up on Wolverine Lake. Won't be back until really late on Sunday."

Why I told Clay this, giving him information where Shelley was, I wasn't sure. Perhaps I thought that by telling Clay Shelley was out of town, I had actually put some physical distance between her and him, and that by creating this distance I had made her safe from him. I can't say that this was a rational response, but I wanted desperately to protect Shelley from Clay and Clay from himself, and that is what I came up with at the time. It wasn't much, wasn't anything actually, but this is what popped out. I must have realized that Shelley would be in danger when she got back on Sunday because I started thinking of ways Clay could hide from the law if it went after him for killing Will, thinking if he thought he was safe he wouldn't feel he'd have to go after Shelley. I was turning over a couple of possibilities in my mind, none of which sounded very good, when Clay interrupted my thinking.

"Well, I guess it can wait until I get back from Florida," he said, stuffing the stack of papers into a manila envelope. "Say, you want some tea and some fresh cinnamon buns? Took them out of the oven just thirty minutes ago."

Clay's casual decision to postpone going after Shelley shocked me after he had just been so intent on getting rid of her. He wasn't making any sense, wasn't being rational, I thought. But then the thought struck me: What was rational from Clay's perspective? He shouldn't kill Shelley because he was close to her, but if he believed Shelley would put him on death row, then it would be logical for him to want to do away with her. But she could spill the beans on him anytime in the next week, so it would be illogical for him to wait. I was trying to make sense of Clay's abrupt change of direction when he started talking about his reunion again. That derailed my effort to understand his thought process.

"I don't want to leave my car at the bus depot all week while I'm in Florida. I know, just know, some kid will mess with it just for fun but I don't know what else to do. Hey, would you like some tea?" he repeated. "There're clean cups in the cupboard."

I got up from the table and headed to the cupboard. Clay's decision to postpone for at least a week killing Shelley must have provided me with some relief as my mind was almost clear by the time I reached the cupboard. So that my mind would have the opportunity to completely return to its normal speed, I took my time selecting a cup.

After a moment had passed, with my head in the cupboard, I spoke. "Say, I've got nothing going on tomorrow, free all day. I can run you over to Middleton and pick you up when you get back. You're getting back on Friday, right? We can check the bus schedule for your return when we get to Middleton so I'll know when to come pick you up. And I can take care of Mollie, too."

"Hey, Frankie. That would be great. Save me a lot of worry. Can you come over around 10:30 tomorrow morning?"

"You tell me you'll have a cinnamon bun for me, I'll be here at 10:00 a.m." My head was still in the cupboard, staring right at an entire row of cups.

"Sure will, ol' buddy, sure will. I'll be taking 'em out of the oven right at 10:00 tomorrow. Give you enough calories to get to Middleton and back."

"That works for me," I said, taking a cup out of the cupboard and pouring me some tea. "Hey, Clay. I just remembered, I've got to get some needles for Lucille. I'll be in big trouble if I don't get her those needles," I said, putting down my cup and picking up my coat.

Clay responded by repeating his offer of cinnamon buns and telling me to take my tea with me. I couldn't say what the expression on his face was; I hadn't looked at him since I'd walked over to the cupboard. Still holding the cup, I opened the door and stepped outside. The tea went into the flower bed next to the back steps.

Driving home, I wondered if I had an ulterior motive in taking Clay to Middleton. I couldn't think of one at the time. The old saying of "Keep your friends close but your enemies closer" crossed my mind. But Clay wasn't my enemy; he was my best friend, had been for sixty-some years. All I was doing was giving my best friend a lift, simple as that, I told myself.

As I turned into my street, Lucille pulled out of the driveway. She lowered her window as I rolled to a stop next to her.

"I'm headed over to Harriet's. How's Clay?"

How was Clay? Forty years I've been married to that woman, and right now I had no idea how to answer her.

"Frank, close your mouth. It's so wide open you're gonna freeze your tonsils off. What's Clay up to?"

"He wants me to drive him over to Middleton tomorrow to catch a bus. He's got a Marine reunion in Florida he's going to for a week."

"Well, that's nice. You two will have lots of time to chat on the way over to Middleton; although I can't see you'll have anything new to talk about, the amount of time the two of you spend together these days. There's chicken soup on the stove. You can have it all; Shelley's off to camp for a week. Oh, Ray from the garage called. Your pickup's done. You can pick it up any time."

Lucille rolled up her window and reached for the gear shift. She stopped and rolled her window down a crack.

"And you might try cleaning up the kitchen. It looks like a teenager cooked all weekend in there with his parents out of town. I don't know what has gotten into you lately. You used to be so neat, and now I can't keep up with the messes you make."

"I'll get right on that kitchen," I said to the back of my wife's car as it turned onto the street.

I pulled into Leonard's driveway and parked his truck there. I left the key in the ignition and walked across his yard to my back door.

Chapter 12
What's Frank to Do?

I took a bowl of soup out to my shop and started a fire in the wood stove. I sat in a recliner I'd got from a yard sale and held the bowl of soup in my lap, thinking about Clay, trying to put everything into perspective. I didn't quite trust the conclusion I'd reached in Clay's kitchen—that he would harm Shelley. Maybe I didn't feel comfortable relying on a decision reached in a state of shock. Or maybe the sixty-plus years I've known this guy told me I had to take one final look. I found a half-full yellow legal pad and a ball point pen that worked, and put these on a bench within easy reach.

I started with the proposition he wouldn't kill Shelley; that was just inconceivable. I wrote that on the legal pad, and then to ensure I would remain open-minded, put a question mark after it. She was just a little girl, I thought, and they were really close. He may be going around the bend, nuttier than a fruitcake, but he wasn't a cold-blooded killer. I was working that idea over pretty hard, spinning out a scenario in my mind that had Clay getting loonier or loonier until someone committed him, all without touching a hair on Shelley's head. I'd gone a ways down that road, well on the way to convincing myself that Shelley was in no real danger of harm, and the major fact pushing me down this road was Clay's feelings for Shelley. I could tell he was really fond of her by the way he treated her and the things he said about her. And he himself told me he was fond of her, this coming from a guy who never expressed his feelings about anyone else, leastways not to me. That by itself told me Clay thought the world of Shelley.

I was feeling pretty good about coming to a solution to this problem when the image of Clay beating Mollie with the rebar flashed in my mind. The relief I had been feeling was sucked right out of me by that picture. Clay had had Mollie for over fifteen years, more than twice as long as he had known Shelley, and Mollie was always at his side. You rarely saw one without the other. And then I thought about Will and Clay methodically beating him to death, as well. I wrote "Mollie" under the first sentence on the legal pad, and on the next line down I put Will's name.

I could go to the police, I thought, and started turning that idea over in my head. I put that down on the pad as a new proposition, ending the sentence with another question mark. I don't think I could sell the idea, Clay wanting to kill Shelley, given Clay's reputation in town, unless I had some pretty solid proof. And the only proof I had was Will's body at the bottom of that well. I spun out how that conversation would go. The police would want to know how I knew about the body in the well. I wasn't certain I could successfully make up a story that didn't involve me. I think that when I got to the point in the story about Will's body being tipped into the well, I couldn't leave my part out without sounding guilty. At least I wasn't sure I could. And who knows what Clay might say once the police started questioning him. Clay was right about one thing, I didn't want to be up in front of Hanging Harry. He wouldn't bat an eye about letting the prosecutor charge me jointly with Clay in killing Will. Even if the charge got reduced to Accessory after the Fact because I helped Clay dispose of the body, Harry would make sure I did hard time, and lots of it.

Why had I gone after that boat? It's not like I really needed it. We had got along fine just renting boats, Clay and I. I just wanted to own a boat, to have one I called my own, to see it in my backyard whenever I went outside. What a lousy reason, I thought, to end up in this . . . I couldn't think of the word that would accurately describe where I was. "Mess" seemed too trivial; "situation" did not carry with it any emotion. "Disastrous predicament" came closest.   But that is what happened to other people, people like my clients who had dropped their problems on my desk, expecting me to find a solution. But I couldn't see any solution here. I started to take a mouthful of soup; my spoon came up empty. I looked down at the bowl sitting in my lap; it, too, was empty. I had absolutely no recollection of eating the soup, and Lucille makes a dynamite chicken soup.

I stood up and put the bowl on the work bench. The calendar caught my eye, and I flipped over a page to the correct month. Automatically I wrote down on the first Wednesday of November, *Clay to Middleton, leave at 10:30 a.m.* Hanging on the right side of this calendar were five calendars on a nail, and next to that stack was another set of five and next to that another set. All down that wall and around the corner were calendars hanging on the wall, five to a nail. Absent-mindedly, I counted the stacks. There were nine in all. It was a habit I started as a teenager, probably inherited from my mother, writing down on a calendar various events and then keeping the calendars as some sort of diary. I kept the calendars through college, and when Lucille and I moved out of the apartment we rented when we first married and into this house, I unpacked the box they were in and started hanging them in my shop. Whenever Clay and I would get into a debate about when something or other happened, we would consult these calendars. One time we were working through a half case of beer on a Saturday afternoon, listening to a baseball game on the radio, and we went through all of them. Clay's name was on every month of every calendar except for the thirteen months he was in Vietnam in the late '60s. Sometimes his name appeared only once in a month, but mostly it was there three or four times.

I made some coffee in the electric coffee pot I had in the shop and got some milk out of the motel refrigerator Clay and I had rescued from the dump. Tools littered the workbench, and I set to work on straightening that up. I hadn't swept the floor in a while, so I grabbed a broom and a dust pan and attacked the floor. I opened the dozen or so gallon paint cans in the corner to see if the paint in them was any good, then pitched the bad ones into the trash container. I found a bunch of knives in a drawer and sharpened them. Some, I hadn't used in twenty years, and probably never would use, but I sharpened them anyway. I grabbed the hose to wash down the floor and then realized it was too cold; the water would freeze on the floor, and I would have created an ice rink. I looked around the shop; I'd never seen it this squared away, short of painting the walls there was nothing more to do. I caught sight of three stick figures made out of pipe cleaners Shelley had created last month. How she found these pipe cleaners I had no idea; I hadn't seen them in years. I probably pushed them out of the way behind a bunch of other junk when I gave up smoking a pipe more than three decades ago; couldn't stand the filthy habit anymore; a guy would be crazy to smoke. I held the stick figures in my hand and sat down heavily in the recliner. I looked over at the legal pad. Maybe, I hoped, someone had come into the shop when my back was turned and written down the answer. But nothing was there except what I had written, the question marks dominating the page.

It must have been mid-afternoon when I got up and walked the two blocks to Ray's to retrieve my pickup. I settled up with him and then took a trip. I couldn't tell how or when I arrived at the decision. It was as if I were traveling down a perfectly straight road, but it turns out the road isn't straight; it has a very slight bend. And the bend is so slow and gentle you don't realize you're around it until you are.

Chapter 13
Back in the Gravel Pit

"Why are you going in here?" Clay asked as I turned off the highway and onto the dirt road leading to the gravel pit. I had gotten over to Clay's a little before 10:00 in the morning to make sure we had plenty of time to get to Middleton. I was balancing a cinnamon bun on one knee and holding a travel cup filled with coffee.

"It will be another hour before we get to the restrooms at the bus station," I replied.

"Thought you took care of that before we left," Clay said. "You need to get your prostate augured out like I did. It'll do wonders for you."

"I'll take your medical views under advisement."

"What's with your shotgun in the rack?"

"My guess is there'll be some geese coming off Wilbur's wheat fields this afternoon, heading to those ponds of his out there on MacArthur Road. I'm thinking I just might swing by there on my way back after dropping you off at the bus station. I could get lucky, given the way this rainstorm is heading. Those clouds should push the geese down into shotgun range."

"Make sure you leave some for seed," Clay said, chuckling.

Both of us were silent for a moment, and then Clay spoke up. "Sure brings back fond memories, the old gravel pit, doesn't it?"

I knew what he was thinking. The gravel pit located two miles outside our home town of Springdale held a lot of memories for the two of us. Not yet thirteen, we rode our bikes here to smoke Camel cigarettes Clay'd lifted from the front seat of his uncle's car. We drank our first illicit beer here from a six-pack liberated from a 4th of July party at my house. And it was in this very gravel pit, on a hot August night between our junior and senior years in high school, we found out what girls were all about. That night is still vivid in my mind's eye. The girls were from Bridgetown, a wheat-farming community ten miles away, and had driven to Springdale that evening because there was absolutely nothing to do in Bridgetown. They found Clay and me sitting on the hood of my parents' car in the parking lot of the local drive-in at the edge of town, two teenagers bored out of their minds with life in a small town.

I drove the quarter mile or so off the highway into the gravel pit, not saying a word. Neither did Clay. I guessed he was thinking about all our good times here. That's not what I was thinking. The pickup rolled to stop between two huge piles of gravel.

Clay got out of the passenger side, saying, "I guess I'll join you."

I got out my side, pulling the shotgun off the rack as I did. Clay didn't see that; his back was to me.

I hesitated for a moment to give Clay time, and rounded the tailgate of the pickup just as he was finishing up and turning around to face me.

"What's with the shotgun? There're no geese here."

"The gun's not for geese, Clay. It's for you."

"Oh," said Clay softly.

Neither of us spoke for a moment, and then Clay did. "It's about Shelley, right?" Clay kept on talking, first about the weather, then asking me what I was going to do about his body, then arguing it wasn't right I was choosing Shelley over him. The last made me angry, and I fired back at him.

"Yeah," I said. "You're right, Clay, it's about Shelley." I went on. "I used to think it was pride that kept you from asking for help, but it wasn't. It wasn't pride; it was fear. You were afraid to ask for help because you would have to admit you were losing it; you were getting old, and you weren't gonna live forever. And you couldn't bring yourself to face that, so you tried to fool everyone into thinking you were just the same as always, but the only person you fooled was yourself."

"Counselor," Clay said, "it sounds like you're making a closing argument for the defense. You're just trying to convince yourself you had no hand in this. But you're the one who got me to take those pills. My best friend, and you doped me up."

"I was trying to take care of you, trying to help you. What are you talking about?"

"Trying to help me, or help yourself? Yeah, now I see what happened here, see real clearly. You didn't want to be by yourself, wanted me to be around, just like I always was. You looked down the road and saw yourself walking all by yourself, all alone, and you got scared, real scared. You couldn't bear the thought of going on without me because we'd always been together. That's why you gave me Hal's pills, so you wouldn't be alone, but you didn't tell me I had to keep taking them. You were afraid if you told me that, I wouldn't start, so you hid that from me. But last night, after I got home, after the guy, when I was feeling normal I got curious and went on the Web, read all about Miazannon and about how you shouldn't get off it once you start. But you didn't tell me that, you the lawyer and all. And my best friend. That guy—what's his name? —Will. Will would still have been alive if you hadn't given me those pills. Would have been able to bury his wife just like the two of them planned."

"You would've killed Will anyway; you were headed in that direction."

"Maybe not, Frankie, maybe not. I didn't go after that kid in the street, remember. Never hurt anyone before, before you gave me that poison Just a dog, an animal, that's all, not the same thing. You wanted things to be the same forever, but nothing's forever, Frankie, nothing's forever. You should've let me go, Frankie, should have let me go."

"I don't need you. I've got Lucille to grow old with." I know I didn't sound convincing.

"Wives aren't the same as best friends, not the same at all."

"At least I didn't kill anyone," I retorted.

"You're about to," he shot back.

I hesitated for a moment, trying to absorb what Clay had just said. "I'm not going after some totally innocent seven-year-old girl. You could've let her go. She's got the rest of her life ahead of her. You've already lived your life." It was the best I could come up with.

"I've got life ahead of me, lots of life. She's too young to know what she'd be missing, but not me. Not me, I know what I'd be missing. You'd do the same as me, Frankie, if you were in my shoes. Just the same as me."

I didn't say anything, just sighted down the barrel at him. There was a terrific roar of thunder followed immediately by a brilliant flash of lightning. We both jumped. Rain came down hard, pelting us both.

"A guy could catch his death of cold out here," Clay said, a slight smile sliding across his face. Good ol' Clay, always got something funny to say at the weirdest time.

"It wasn't the boat that got us here, Clay, not the boat at all."

"Oh, you mean Helen, my dentist. If she hadn't got pregnant, I would've been sitting in the dentist chair yesterday. Wouldn't have been in that guy's barn. We always said sex would get us in trouble." Clay chuckled again.

"That's not what I mean, Clay. You know what I mean. You could've gotten some help. Could've, but you didn't." I was repeating myself, a signal to me that I was running out of arguments, things to say, and the conversation would shortly be ending. But it didn't; instead it took a turn I didn't see coming.

Clay was silent for a moment. Maybe he was out of things to say, too. But then his ears started wiggling. "What are you gonna do about her, Frankie? Will's wife. What was her name? Oh, yeah, Annie. What are you gonna do about Annie?"

"I don't have to worry about her; she'll be gone in a week."

"That's what I mean. She's lying there now, on that old couch, too weak to move, even to get a drink of water. And in pain, excruciating pain because she hasn't had any marijuana today. She's waiting for Will to come through the door, to be with her at the end, to carry her to her grave when she dies. What are you gonna to do to help her, to make her last moments on this earth good and decent and peaceful?"

"Don't lay that on me, Clay. You're the reason Will's not walking through that door."

"Yeah, but you're taking me out of the picture now, and that makes her your deal. Or is she just collateral damage as far as you're concerned now? You used to be better than that."

I started to fire back, and there was a lot I was going to say when Clay interrupted me. He had a head of steam up now.

"She saw you, too, Frankie. Shelley saw you help me tip the guy into the well. She was peeking out the barn door when you grabbed his leg and helped me up-end him into the well. You were looking into the well and didn't see her, but I did. Will was still alive when he went into the well, and the fall probably broke his neck. The autopsy will show that. You're in this deal as deep as I am. You better be thinking about that. About what you're gonna say when you're stand-ing up in front of Hanging Harry." Clay paused, his ears slowly wiggling.

"Say, Frankie, that friend of Shelley's, what's her name? Oh, yeah, Jennifer. Her mom's a deputy sheriff, right? As much as little girls talk, I bet it won't be long now before Shelley starts talking to Jennifer about what she saw at the well. And I wouldn't be surprised if Jennifer runs right home and tells her mom."

Clay was smiling at me now as he kept on talking.

"You know, Frankie, my not being around won't look good for you. Ol' Harry gonna think that I hightailed it out of here because something bad happened out there; I disap-peared because I didn't want to get caught. That's like I'm admitting I'm guilty. And as close as everyone knows we are;

people will think we were in it together. And of course with me under that block of concrete, I won't be around to tell people it was just me. Harry's gonna want to stick someone pretty hard with this, and you're gonna be the only one in front of him. He's gonna give you both barrels."

"You didn't see anything. You were looking into the well, too. Besides, you said he was dead, you did. I remember clearly you said he was dead," I shot back.

"She saw both of us, buddy boy, you better believe that. As for Will, well I lied to you about him being dead because I couldn't get him in the well myself and needed your help. Knew you wouldn't help me if you thought he was alive, so I told you he was dead. So what are you gonna do, sue me?"

He started chuckling at that, and then the chuckling grew into laughter. I told him to stop laughing, but he just kept on laughing harder and harder, like he couldn't stop. There was only one way to make him stop. I pulled the shotgun back hard against my shoulder to lessen the recoil.

I'm in the front-end loader now, letting the engine idle before I shut it down. The weather has moved in. Rain is hitting the roof of the cab hard, and the thunder and lightning are almost continuous. In a moment the tracks of the loader going to and from the concrete blocks will be obliterated by the rain. I'm smoking a Camel cigarette that I'd found in a pack lying against the windshield of the loader. The cigarette tastes good, and I enjoy the effect of nicotine; it really relaxes me. The scene at the well flows into in my mind.

In my mind's eye, my right arm is wrapped around Will's stomach, and my other hand is grasping the knee of his left leg. I need more leverage so I reach lower on his leg and grab his ankle, my head turning toward the barn as I do. Shelley is standing in the barn door, watching us, watching me. That's how I remember the scene now. But it's kinda funny, 'cause I don't recall remembering it that way on the drive back to town or last night at home before I drifted off to sleep. Last night I think I remembered seeing Shelley for the first time only after I had been staring into the well for a while, looking up only when Clay started honking the horn. But now that doesn't seem quite right.

I look through the windshield of the front-end loader, past the bucket, over to the jumble of concrete blocks. There's a hole there, between two of the blocks. The hole looks to be about three feet deep and five feet long. Bet a seven-year-old would fit in there real neat. All a guy would have to do would be to roll one of those blocks over; nothing would show. Wouldn't take but a minute. I shut off the engine, climb down from the loader, head for my pickup.

Afterword

Thanks for buying my book. If you enjoyed it, please tell a **friend**. Also, highly appreciated would be putting an honest review on Amazon and on Goodreads. Reviews help other readers locate books they might like.

If you have any questions about this story, like where I got the idea or how the story developed, feel free to contact me on my website, *http://robertscottwriter.wordpress.com/*, or on Twitter @robbiehscottjr.

And if you want to know what happened between Frank and Shelley, you will have to read my next novel, *How Jennifer Sees It*. This book will be out some time during the second half of 2016, and I will be announcing its publication date on my website.

The Fresh Ink Group

Publishing
Free Memberships
Free Stories, Essays, Articles
Free-Story Newsletter
Writing Contests

Books
E-books
Amazon Bookstore

Authors
Editors
Artists
Professionals
Publishing Services
Publisher Resources

Readers' Forum
Blogs
Social Media

www.FreshInkGroup.com

Email: info@FreshInkGroup.com

**The Fresh Ink Group is a proud member of
The Coalition of Independent Authors and Publishers**

DANCE OF THE LIGHTS

By Stephen Geez

Frank relishes fast success and early retirement, but struggling to preserve his life's work thrusts him into a desperate battle to protect the people he cares about most.

Beverly seeks a new beginning in Tarpon Springs—until those she trusts steal control of her destiny, forcing a fight for her very survival.

All twelve-year-old Kevin wants is attention from the only man he respects, yet murder and the wrenching indifference of a callous legal system toward one vulnerable child proves even friendship might never be enough.

Riven by tragedy, consumed by grief, all three must confront the wondrous possibility that our indelible bonds may somehow transcend even death, that a cherished soul truly can find the way back.

Only together might this improbable family dare embrace their own brand of unexpected love, that infinite potential to achieve more than any one person can alone. Through it all, they are teased by the mystery of those dancing lights, a million pinpoints in every imaginable color swirling to form brilliant images of extraordinary lives.

www.FreshInkGroup.com
ISBN: 978-1-936442-00-3

BEEN THERE, NOTED THAT:

Essays In Tribute To Life

Observations, Inspiration, Remembrance, & Noteworthies To Share

By Stephen Geez

The simple lives of everyday people in a mundane world prove extraordinary in this collection of 54 personal-experience essays by novelist Stephen Geez. The eclectic mix of memoir, commentary, humor, and appreciation covers a wide range of topics, each beautifully illustrated by artists and photographers from the Fresh Ink Group. Geez catches what many of us miss, then considers how we might all share the most poignant of lessons. *Been There, Noted That* aims to reveal who we are, examine where we've been, and discover what we dare strive to become.

www.FreshInkGroup.com
ISBN: 978-1-936442-05-8

COURAGEOUS LADY

By Mark Allen North

In the first novel of The Lady Trilogy, auburn-haired beauty Leigh West travels to Alaska's majestic and mysterious Tongass National Forest in search of self-discovery and harmony with nature. In her journal, she chronicles all she learns from native Tlingit tribesmen, the cunning wolves and beligerent brown bears, and the transforming seasons of the region's glorious landscape. It is through Native American spirituality that she sparks new passion within herself, a new appreciation for the physical world, and a life filled with love.

www.FreshInkGroup.com
ISBN: 978-1-936442-12-6

www.ingramcontent.com/pod-product-compliance
Lightning Source LLC
Chambersburg PA
CBHW020309150626
46552CB00022B/2410